MW00942163

FOLKLORE

Mitch Sebourn

Folklore
© 2017 by Mitch Sebourn

Cover design and photographs
© 2017 by Mitch Sebourn

ALSO BY MITCH SEBOURN

Watershed

Sleight of Hand

Hawks & Handsaws

Inner Sequence

Lamentation

The Hawthorn Room

Toklat's Daughter

1

DEAN MITCHELL WAS THE ONLY lawyer in town. He'd thought about advertising as such but decided it would be an invitation for competition. Put that truth on the door and watch one of the big shots in Harrison open a satellite office across the street, and he couldn't have that. Dean Mitchell, Attorney at Law, had come to the hills to be the one and only.

Ellingwood was four hundred strong, and shrinking. But Dean stayed busy, thanks in part to the strong presence he'd established in Harrison. He made a good living. He fed his ego. And he was his own boss. Was he happy? Hell no. But his unhappiness was no fault of his setting or profession. He was simply a wretch and considered himself wise for being aware of it.

He was sipping coffee and wondering why—why everything—when a black Civic pulled up in front of his office, right on time. His first potential new client of the day, Savannah Golding, slung her purse over her right shoulder and checked her look in the window. She was going on fifty but looked closer to forty, despite her fondness for cigarettes and alcohol.

She entered his office and the corners of her mouth pulled up a bit—he wouldn't quite call it a smile—and he motioned her back to his desk.

They took their places, Dean in his fake leather chair and Savannah in the little plastic one across from him, and Savannah kicked things off with the bluntness that was so typical of her: "I'm divorcing him. But you know that."

She was much too happy, Dean thought, and really, he wanted no part of it.

He clicked open a pen, flipped to a clean page in his legal pad, and wrote her name at the top. Then came the basics: When they were married (May, 2005), where they lived (Ellingwood, the whole time), children (one), expected children (none, dear God). And then, of course, the big question: "Why are you divorcing him?"

Dean Mitchell expected the answer to be as blunt as usual. But for a moment, she simply looked away, back toward the door, and watched the snow flurries that had just begun to fly.

"He's never been violent." She looked at her lap. "But things haven't been good for us. You know. We basically haven't communicated in a month. I never see him. He knows I don't love him."

Dean didn't want to think about it. He tried to focus on nothing but his writing as he scribbled down a few words.

Savannah said: "And our daughter. I haven't heard from her since last week. Thursday, I think. It's *Monday* now. I blame him."

"Is she okay?"

"I don't know. I haven't heard from her."

"Where is he?"

"He's been working out at the Evenware House. I assume he stays out there. The old lady is paying him to tear it down."

"Tear it down?"

The half smile returned. "It's appropriate, isn't it? Anyway…"

SHE DIDN'T STAY LONG AFTER they finished talking. She simply wrote him a check, smiled sweetly (her *full* smile), and said, "Thank you."

This was not at all what he'd expected, but maybe that wasn't a bad thing. Maybe Nathaniel Golding wouldn't fight this divorce at all. Maybe the whole thing would go smoothly.

After she left, he sat at this desk, drumming his fingers and thinking about what all she'd said. She no longer loved her husband, Nathaniel. He was a nobody handyman, void of ambition, content to roof sheds and renovate trailers and spend his evenings burning through Natural Light watching Netflix; that she'd ever reproduced with him was depressingly remarkable, and his lackadaisical attitude toward life had "rubbed off" on Marion, their daughter. She'd never considered college, just gone straight to work at the gift shop in the ranger station north of town. ("And that old black man,

Robert, she works for is so sweet, but Dean… Does she intend to *stay* there?")

Savannah, frankly, was a snob. She'd moved to Arkansas from Memphis and had always thought she was too good for the area. Why was she here? "I wanted out of the city. I met Nathaniel. I just knew I loved him. He was something totally different, like a stupid fantasy. Till he wasn't."

This was all fine, Dean Mitchell thought. Very typical, actually. If not for love that wasn't love and the children it usually spawned, small town lawyers would struggle to pay their light bills. But what was this about Nathaniel staying out at the old Evenware House? Surely not. The Evenware House was a ruin; the Evenwares hadn't lived out there since the eighties or nineties, at least. Who could stay out there for any prolonged period? Surely Savannah was mistaken, or for whatever reason seeing if she could make his job just a *little bit* more complicated. But why would she do that?

It didn't matter. He had work to do. Not just drafting Savannah's divorce complaint, either. That would take all of ten or fifteen minutes. No, he had several tasks to complete today. Deeds to draft, a power of attorney to draft; he had to call Emily up in the prosecutor's office in Harrison, had to call Judge Benedict's office and set a hearing date for a strung out fool who'd attempted to steal a trampoline… and if he was totally honest with himself, he needed to call and set up a meeting with, speak of the devil, Mary Evenware herself. He dreaded it. Hopefully her son would be there to help the communication, because Mary Evenware seldom knew who she was and was getting worse all the time. Yes, he dreaded it, but when he faced reality, he knew that the last few months had yielded nothing but the minimum, just enough piddling crap to pay the bills and stock the refrigerator. Mary Evenware was worth at least a couple of million. He wanted in on her estate, and he had to make that call.

He'd make it today.

He'd get a little drafting done this morning, including Savannah's complaint, have lunch with his wife… maybe go see Mary this afternoon.

If he were lucky, maybe he'd leave with a check. Or cash.

KATELYN MET HIM AT THE Painted Lady, the only restaurant in town. It was a one-room cafe owned by Riley Saunders, who was better known as the Ellingwood constable. The Painted Lady, the post office, and Dean Mitchell's building were all that remained of Ellingwood's "downtown." The other three buildings—a gas station, a hardware store, and an antique shop—had been destroyed during 1985's Christmas Day tornado.

Katelyn did a decent job of acting like she was in a good mood, but the truth was there, all over her. Dean had been married to her for eleven years. She wasn't happy with him, hadn't been in years. She'd grown to despise his profession and "what it was doing to him." She'd thought getting out of Little Rock would do him good, but Ellingwood had apparently just "inflated his ego" which had wiped out what sense of "humanity" he had left. Such were her thoughts.

5

Just last night, she'd accused him of never being romantic, probably being unfaithful, and quashing her creativity: Katelyn was a songwriter. Or, she wanted to be.

Sometimes, Dean Mitchell thought, the woman acted like she'd give up everything they had if he'd just quit work and sit and listen to her play her goddamned guitar. He didn't *mean* to be disinterested… he just didn't give a damn and couldn't fake it.

"Did she actually show up?" Katelyn said. "Savannah, I mean."

"She showed."

"Why does she want a divorce?"

"She's too good for him." He sipped his Pepsi, hoping the answer was enough and knowing she was not a fool. "You know that."

AFTER LUNCH, DEAN MITCHELL RETURNED to his office and sent emails, organized his desk, and called Mary Evenware. Her son, Lewis, picked up and said hello.

"This is Dean Mitchell." He sat down on the front edge of his desk. "Your mother contacted me two weeks ago about a trust. I've got time this afternoon to come by."

"You're welcome to come by, Mr. Mitchell," Lewis said. "She has a check here for the first third of the amount, like you agreed, but I don't know how much you'll get from her. Today isn't a good day."

"If tomorrow would be better…"

6

"There's no guarantee of that, unfortunately. Do you have enough information to get started?"

"I do. She'd been writing things down."

"Then yes, see her. She asks about it. She worries you've forgotten."

Dean was not going to argue with anybody who had a check written. He told Lewis he'd be right over and drove south on 307, the only main road through town, until he reached the ranch house at the intersection with Evenware Road on the right. Keep going on Evenware Road till it narrowed and became a nearly impassable driveway, and you'd eventually reach the *old* Evenware property, where Savannah had claimed Nathaniel was spending his days… and nights.

Dean had never been out there, wasn't even sure his truck would make it.

And, there was no check out there.

Lewis met him at the front door and said Mary was in the kitchen, anxious to talk to him.

"She's better, then?" Dean said. "I'm glad to hear that."

Lewis was a homely, awkward fellow, the kind of adult child you'd expect to be living with his elderly mother. Just now, he flashed Dean a glance that said no, probably not *better*, but certainly *insistent*.

Dean followed the man into the kitchen and found Mary sitting beside a window at a small round table. She was stirring a cup of coffee and studying the khaki-colored drink intently, until she heard her lawyer speak her name. Then, the old lady raised her head and beamed and told him to sit down.

"How are you, Mr. Mitchell?" she said.

Dean told her he was doing fine, he just wanted to get some more information from her about the documents he was drafting.

"The trust? The trust. I'd almost forgotten. No, I *did* forget."

Lewis leaned against the counter behind her, shaking his head.

Dean simply needed a few moments of clarity from the woman. She'd been remarkably sharp just a couple of weeks ago. Do these things really happen so quickly?

He opened his briefcase and withdrew a legal pad and pen, and Mary Evenware focused again on her coffee.

"Would you like coffee, Mr. Mitchell?" Lewis said. "Soda? Water?"

Dean told him he was fine, thank you.

Mary looked again and exclaimed surprise that her lawyer was here. "How are you?"

Again, Dean said he was fine. He also accepted that this was not going to happen. Not today.

"I was just stopping in to say hello, Ms. Evenware." He tucked his things away and clasped the case. "I hope you're doing well."

Mary Evenware beamed and said it was a great day.

Dean stood and said to Lewis. "We'll talk some other time."

He was stepping out of the room when Mary said, "I'm paying somebody to take care of the old house. Don't go out there now. The berries are toxic."

Dean looked straight at Lewis.

"She didn't want me out there, either," Lewis said.

8

2

WHEN DEAN MITCHELL ARRIVED HOME that evening, his dinner was on the table—spaghetti and garlic bread—and the soft strumming of an acoustic guitar was audible from Katelyn's upstairs "studio." The presence of food with the absence of his wife was not an anomaly.

She probably still loved him, but she wanted no part of him.

Dean Mitchell supposed his thoughts were similar. Katelyn was a talented songwriter, as talented in that particular art, Dean had to admit, as he was at practicing law. And in the early days of their marriage, in Little Rock, they'd offered one another new perspectives; they'd balanced their individual viewpoints. Time, however, revealed that life was expensive, and law paid more than songwriting. After Dean pointed this out, Katelyn suggested they move to Nashville, where she might make "connections." Dean scoffed; he'd *just passed the Arkansas bar* two years ago; he was *not* moving out of state. Compromise? Head to the hills. They'd both enjoy the scenery; they'd both enjoy cheaper living; and Dean, secretly, had become very overwhelmed by his Little Rock gig. Carrying a briefcase and working out of the fourteenth story of a glass building made him feel important, but he was the low guy; he was doing the work of three lawyers while those above him golfed. Katelyn wanted to move? Glory to God, he was all about it, just not out of state. Living cheaper would benefit them both, he argued, and she could write her songs anywhere. That's what the Internet was for.

So here they were.

Dean took a beer from the refrigerator, ate his supper, dwelled a bit longer in the past, and wondered if he hated himself. He decided he actually *didn't*. He was simply angry. And he had a right to be! Katelyn lived perpetually in a fairytale, believing that geography was the sole reason she wasn't raking in cash for her songs; she blamed *him* for her struggles, which angered him, which caused him to spend more time at work… or with Savannah Golding… and then Katelyn, again, blamed *him*.

No wonder he and Savannah had joked that night about killing their spouses.

Dean had to admit, he'd been a little bit spooked, and still was, that he hadn't been totally joking.

He pushed his plate away, sat back, and sipped his beer.

One of his wife's songs had been floating around Nashville for over a year. The likes of Tim McGraw and

10

Billy Currington had *supposedly* given it more than a passing glance, and a big name from the nineties—Mark Chesnutt, Dean believed—had *supposedly* been sitting on it for six months.

Dean wondered what she was working on now. Anything? Or was she simply up there ignoring him?

After he rinsed off his plate and put it in the dishwasher, he went to the bottom of the stairs and listened.

The music eventually stopped. The only sound was the neighbor's yowling husky, Doris.

But Katelyn did not come downstairs.

Dean Mitchell knew what that meant, and there was no point in arguing.

HE DROVE TO HIS OFFICE slowly, silently. Snow flurries emerged in slow motion from the darkness and danced amidst his headlight beams.

He parked in the wide alleyway between his office and The Painted Lady, grabbed a gym bag he'd packed with various items from his passenger seat, and went around to the exterior staircase at the back of the building. The room above his office was only accessible from back here. And because of its low ceiling, it wasn't obvious from the road that it existed at all. Back during their first year here, Dean had considered renting this room out. Now, it was too precious to him; that very few knew about it only added to its value. He'd rather come here and be alone than go to the End Zone, Ellingwood's only bar, and put up with the ruckus of drunken fools shouting over ballgames.

11

This cold and empty little room with one window and surely a few dozen mice was much more peaceful.

He locked the door behind him and sat down in the room's only piece of furniture, a frayed armchair he'd found in a ditch a few months back. He sat down, retrieved a paperback novel and a bottle of Coors from the gym bag, and attempted to settle in. His plan was to pass the evening and night away here and leave about eleven or midnight, after his wife was surely in bed.

But he realized, after reading and re-reading the same page in the paperback two or three times, that he could not relax. And he realized, too, that he could not stop thinking about the Evenware House. How interesting that both Savannah Golding and Mary Evenware had mentioned it to him. That uninhabitable ruin out in the middle of the woods! Abandoned sometime after… Mary's husband died? Went missing?

Dean Mitchell finished his second beer of the evening, opened the third, set down the paperback, and let his mind go wherever it wished.

BEING AN ADULT, MARION GOLDING, Savannah and Nathaniel's daughter, wouldn't play a huge role in the divorce, if any at all. That was his original thought. But a few beers in, this thought morphed into something else. Because he thought of Savannah, of Nathaniel, thought about how Nathaniel was working for Mary Evenware out at the old house, doing something, tearing it down, something, for God knows why, and yes, it was strange that he'd grown so estranged from his wife that he wasn't coming home at all, as he was basically—

what?—camping out there? Strange, no, downright *weird*. Okay. And so *now* (and wasn't this interesting) Dean moved onto Marion, grownup daughter who just wanted to sell maps and tee shirts at the ranger station, but now she was gone. Savannah had told him she hadn't heard from Marion in several days. Savannah believed, or wanted to believe, that her daughter had grown frustrated with her parents and split town— maybe she'd gone to apply to some colleges! But what if it were something else? Oh God, the places Dean Mitchell's mind was going. He hated himself for grinning about it, but when you're cracking open beer number four, what do you expect?

What if Marion Golding was out at the old Evenware place with her dad? Dean Mitchell had never known Marion, and he didn't really know Nathaniel, either. She could be out there helping him out. Conspiring against her mother? What else? There were possibilities here that would be a *blast* to write into a divorce complaint. *Truly, Dean,* he thought, *you are a sick, sick bastard.*

He decided that, when he was done with this beer, he'd drive out there. He had nothing else to do with this night. He wasn't entirely sober, but he wasn't drunk, either, and he only had a couple of miles of highway to cover before he reached Evenware Road, where there was a *zero* percent chance he'd meet up with a law enforcement officer.

He had to see if Nathaniel Golding was truly out there. And if he was, was he alone?

Less than ten minutes after making this decision, he was turning onto Evenware Road and saying a silent prayer that his truck could handle what was to come. It didn't help his effort that the road was dusted with snow, and the flurries were still coming down. For the first two miles, the terrain was flat and the gravel was packed and smooth. But somewhere between mile two and three, as the woods crept in close and the pathway narrowed, he passed a sign that read ROAD ENDS: PRIVATE PROPERTY, and the path deteriorated as it descended toward the Harrelston Bayou.

Dean Mitchell realized he'd made a mistake. He had no business out here. This wasn't a road anymore; it was a private drive that hadn't been maintained in at least thirty years. He was looking for a place to turn around—to hell with this—when he found himself at a place where the trees retreated from the drive and the landscape flattened, and his headlights revealed a rotted, skeletal corpse of a house. It sat about fifty yards away, across a rugged tundra of rocks and snow.

"No way he's here," Dean Mitchell said.

He dared not drive any closer, as the driveway had faded entirely and he feared he'd damage his truck on some unknown obstacle if he tried to cross the property in the dark.

So he left it where it was and hiked up the lawn. He took his phone out of his pocket and turned on its flashlight before stepping through the jagged, open portal that was the front door.

He tested the floorboards before going too far. And, satisfied that they weren't going to give way beneath him, he set about exploring.

There was nothing to find, of course. The dilapidated building was empty of everything except dirt, cobwebs, scattered trash, and a plant growing up out of the floorboards in a far corner. His thought that there was no way anybody was living out here was confirmed. Or so he thought. Until he spotted the Nissan Frontier parked behind the house.

Dean stood before the broken back window for a moment, staring, his mouth agape. Not only was he now convinced that he was not alone, he somehow also knew that something was terribly wrong.

He pulled himself away from the window and cautiously ascended the staircase he found in the northeast corner of what had once been a den.

Somehow, it was not nearly as cold upstairs, and the unnatural warmth only unnerved him more.

No. He should not be here. It had seemed so fun and amusing, come out here and, what? Catch Nathaniel passed out drunk? With his daughter? What had he thought he was doing? Clearly, he'd been ignorant of how far out this place was, how bad the road was… how bad the *house* was.

I need to know where he is. How do you serve a man with his divorce papers if you don't know where he is?

Foolish. He should not be here. Period.

The warm humidity hung in the air and thickened as he proceeded across a landing, into a small room about the size of a child's bedroom. In here, the humidity was so thick it was visible as a glimmering mist.

And the room stunk. The ripe smell of rot. Death.

He convinced himself to leave, get out, do whatever it took, go back to his office, go back home, sleep the beer off, forget he'd ever been here—but then

15

he saw the splatters on the wall to his left and the heap on the floor directly below it. Nathaniel's body. Dean had never known the man well, but sure, he'd seen him around. And who else would this be, this dried out, sprawled dead thing with various substances leaking out of its head?

Dean retreated into the doorway, and a splinter of wood from the frame caught the side of his neck, just below his left ear. He cursed, staggered, and stepped onto a plank that was not there. He overcompensated in his attempt to not fall completely through the floor. He fell forward and landed face-first on Golding's left shoulder.

The body was damp. Sticky. He wanted to cry out and couldn't. Jesus Christ, what had he done?

I'm okay, he thought, rising, pulling his foot out of the hole in the floor, wiping his face. But he'd dropped his phone, the light was out, and the gash in his neck was bleeding. He put a hand up to the wound, cursed, then knelt down and reached for his phone. Not there, which was ridiculous; it had landed right in front of him! He'd heard it. No way it had fallen through the floor. No way—here it was. Right here.

The clouds broke. Moonlight beamed through cracks in the roof and ceiling. Faint silver illuminated the dampness in the room and contrasted with the corpse on the floor and the darkness that leaked from it.

And there was a shadow of a man, or something *like* a man, on the wall across from him. It wasn't *his* shadow, and it certainly wasn't Nathaniel Golding's.

Nor was it there for more than a second.

Just long enough to drive Dean Mitchell out onto the landing and down the stairs.

3

KATELYN MITCHELL AWOKE AT EIGHT 'o clock the next morning to the sound of the husky, Doris, making her typical racket.

Katelyn was confused, until the previous evening returned to her. She was upstairs in her attic studio, next to her guitar and an empty bottle of wine, dressed in socks, panties, and a half-buttoned flannel shirt. She felt okay, somehow, with only a slight headache, and she almost smiled. She was forty-three, and it had been at *least* ten years since she'd woken up scantly dressed in the middle of a floor, next to a drained bottle of booze.

Almost smiled, but a subtle frown, when she thought about how her circumstances had changed, was much more appropriate. Her friends from college and Little Rock were scattered, and even their minimal, meaningless social media contact was rare. She was a grownup now, a woman; she'd been a little girl then,

18

though Katelyn the brilliant college student (and graduate) had never thought of herself as immature. But it was all about priorities. Young Katelyn was going to change everything, be brilliant, have fun. Now, Grown Katelyn only wanted to make a living doing, hopefully, something she loved. Be married to someone she loved. And she still sometimes hoped for a family.

She'd seen enough to know how unreachable some or all of these modest goals might be. That was the difference. The craft she loved only occasionally paid a bill. She wondered sometimes if she still loved Dean and assumed he'd fallen out of love with her a long time ago, possibly before they ever left Little Rock. And there was the whole *mortality* thing, too. Had Young Katelyn even considered kidney stones, aching joints, miscarriages, constipation, debilitating periods, or breast lumps (which had been benign, thank God)? No, Katelyn thought, smiling. Young Katelyn had been such a naive little nymph.

She propped her Breedlove against a broken Line 6 amp, thinking it was probably a *good* thing she'd drank an entire bottle of wine last night. She'd been furious. At Dean. Mostly at herself. She'd known for weeks he was going to represent Savannah Golding in her divorce, yet after his lunchtime confirmation that he'd met with her and drafted the complaint, it happened anyway—the avalanche of grief, anger, and self-loathing. If not for the wine, who knows what she might've done with the previous evening.

She went downstairs, brushed her teeth, peed, showered, and dressed in a pair of jeans and one of Dean's Dallas Cowboys sweatshirts. It occurred to her, as she stood before the mirror in the master bath, pulling her hair back in a ponytail and studying this sweatshirt that she loved to wear because it was way too big and thus very comfortable, that Dean was not in bed.

No, Dean was *nowhere*.

His absence did not surprise her, and she barely cared. If she had the house to herself all day, then God was indeed good.

She was eating a piece of toast and waiting for a pot of coffee to brew when the doorbell rang.

It was Ellingwood's only law enforcement presence, the constable, Riley Saunders. Riley was a petite yet firm little thing, somewhere around thirty-five. As far as Katelyn knew, she wasn't paid a cent to be the constable; she earned whatever income she had with The Painted Lady, the diner she'd inherited from her parents. Yet, most of those in Ellingwood thought of Riley Saunders *only* as the constable; Riley was almost always in uniform (cargo pants and a buttoned shirt with a constable star on the sleeve) and was not a smothering business owner; The Painted Lady had been in the hands of a capable manager since long before Riley inherited it.

This was the extent of Katelyn's knowledge about Constable Saunders. She'd only ever spoken to her in public, casually. Until today.

Riley was on her porch, smiling pleasantly, hands in the pockets of her Columbia jacket.

Katelyn greeted her pleasantly. Riley returned the greeting and asked if Dean Mitchell was home.

"I haven't seen Dean since yesterday. He left after dinner last night."

Riley said: "I found his truck parked in the alley beside his office. Unfortunately, his office is locked up and dark and a good bit of his truck is hanging out in the highway."

"I imagine he was upset when he left here. He probably drank too much. Did you check upstairs?"

"At his office?"

"You can't tell from the front, but there's a room upstairs. You get there from the back."

"I've lived here my whole life and didn't know that building had a second floor. I guess I've never been around back."

"He doesn't know I know. Sometimes he's not very smart."

KATELYN SHUT THE DOOR AND tried to decide if she should be concerned or merely confused. If concerned, how much? She suddenly regretted everything about last night. She should've been downstairs. She should've waited on him and had dinner with him. There had been many times in which Katelyn's ill feelings toward her husband were grounded in reality and absolutely justified; yesterday, that hadn't been the case. She had *damned* good reasons for wanting him to stay away from Savannah Golding and not even think about working her divorce, but they'd been there, argued that, and her pouting last night had been, at best, overkill.

Had he gone to his escape hole and drank himself into a stupor? That's probably what happened. But why

21

was his truck parked like it was? Had he started drinking before he left the house and driven drunk to his office? She'd never known him to do such a thing. He wasn't a fool. If he had any inclination at all that he was going to inebriate himself, he typically first got to where he was going.

She was, then, concerned and confused.

There was no reason for his truck to be parked halfway out in the highway unless he'd done something out of character, or last night had been very bizarre.

RILEY SAUNDERS RETURNED TO DEAN Mitchell's office and parked her Wrangler directly in front of his building. The traffic cone she'd placed in the street in front of his poorly-parked truck was still there; nobody had hit anything yet.

She proceeded up the alleyway to the back of the building.

From back here, looking up the metal exterior steps she'd never seen before, she could see how there was enough space for an upstairs room. It wasn't nearly as obvious from the front of the building, though Riley now realized this was an illusion caused primarily by the sign and the decorative trim work above the door and window.

Riley also realized, as she stood in the narrow passage between the back of Dean Mitchell's office and a concrete retaining wall, that she'd only been in this building once. She was thirty-five, almost thirty-six, had lived in Ellingwood her entire life, had passed by this building in car and on foot hundreds or thousands of times, and had only been inside it once, and that was back in the late nineties, when she was still a teenager, long before Ellingwood had ever heard of Dean Mitchell, attorney at law.

Back then, this building had housed an accountant's office. Then, a used bookstore (this had lasted approximately three months). Then it had been empty. Then it was a hair salon. After that, empty again, until Mitchell had bought it... almost four years ago. Depressing, Riley thought. It reminded her that she was looking directly at forty, that her parents had been dead for ten years, that she'd been a business owner, unfortunately, for nearly a decade, thanks to cancer and suicide.

Funny, the things that took her back to her parents' deaths. Some things, she thought, you just never accept or get over.

For years, Riley had refused to accept that her dad's lethal cocktail of antidepressants, painkillers, and whiskey had been intentional. Then she got busy. Finished her associates degree. Fixed up The Painted Lady with money her parents had set aside for just that cause. Ran for constable and won, since she was the only one on the ballot. And somewhere in the midst of all this, she accepted it.

Accepted, yes, but sometimes, like now, her eyes still misted up. Yes. Funny the things that take you back. Just standing here, looking up at this building, thinking about the passing of time.

She forced a laugh. No need to cry. There was nothing emotionally heavy about telling Dean Mitchell to move his truck.

She ascended the steps and knocked on the door at the top. Dean Mitchell answered, dressed in what Riley guessed were yesterday's clothes. His eyes were red. His hair matted to his forehead.

She let him study her for a moment and asked if he was okay.

"Yes," he said. "Katie and I argued, so…" He swept his arm into the room as if revealing to her the vast and awesome nature of his hideaway. "You can come in here. It's cold."

"I'm fine," Riley said, "but your truck isn't."

"My truck? It's in the alley, isn't it?"

"Halfway. The back end is out in the highway, you'll need to move it. When did you come here?"

"After I had dinner. I don't know. Six. Seven."

"Were you sober?"

"After dinner?"

"Just whenever you came here."

"Yes, I was sober. I think I had one beer at dinner. I might've drank tea. I don't remember." And then his eyes widened, and he stepped back and sat down on the room's only piece of furniture. "Oh shit."

Riley stepped into the room and shut the door behind her. She thought he would continue on his own, but he simply sat there in silence, staring at the floor, unblinking, picking at what looked like a nasty wound on the side of his neck.

"Were you here all night, Mr. Mitchell?" she said.

"No." His voice was suddenly soft, stuffed with gravel. "I had a silent argument with my wife. Got home, she had me a plate, but she was upstairs. She… You don't care about that. I came here, last night. I

24

parked my truck fine. I drank a beer or two. Three. And I left."

"After drinking beer?"

"I wasn't drunk. That doesn't matter. Slap me, or..." He stood up again, as if his confidence were regained. "I don't care. It doesn't matter. I left. I got hired to represent Savannah Golding in her divorce. She told me she thinks her husband has been staying out at the old Evenware house, and—"

"Staying at the Evenware House?" Riley was suddenly confused and didn't mind showing it. "Why on Earth would he be out there, and what does this have to do with your truck?"

"I'm explaining. You have to let me talk or I can't say it, and I need to say it. You woke me up, and my neck hurts. Just hear me."

Riley motioned for him to continue.

He said: "I'd never been out to the Evenware place. I got curious last night. And you might've heard, or not, but Savannah Golding hasn't heard from Marion—her daughter—since last week sometime. I got to wondering, were they together? Forgive me, but I drove out there. And this is the important part. He was out there. Nathaniel Golding was out there. Dead. In a bedroom upstairs."

"Dead?" Riley was already reaching for her phone. "You found Nathaniel Golding dead? You didn't call 911? You didn't—"

"I didn't even remember being *out there* till about thirty seconds ago. It's coming back to me. I hurt my neck—I scraped it against something. I fell on him and lost my shit. And I ran. I ran all the way back to my truck. When I got in my truck, I tried messing with my phone. But my hands were shaking and the screen's all messed up because I dropped it. So I started back. When I got on the other side of the private property sign, I felt better, and I started wondering if I'd really seen it. I thought maybe I'd spooked myself. I came back here. I told myself I'd have one more drink, close my eyes, and when I woke up, I'd either remember it all, or I'd laugh at myself."

"You're saying you believe you found a dead man—Nathaniel Golding—out on the old Evenware property, and you came back here after that, didn't call for help, and that's when you left your truck half in the street."

"I apologize for my truck. I was frantic and confused. And Riley—Constable—I am a *lawyer*, and pardon me, but a damned good one. There is no *way* I'm lying to you or have anything to hide. Call Sheriff Palmer. That's what I'd do. There's a dead man in that house."

Riley believed him. She also knew she didn't like him, at all.

"Go move your truck, please," she said.

When he was gone, she scrolled down to Sheriff Wilson Palmer's number.

What a damned morning.

4

THE WOUND REFUSED TO HEAL.

Dean Mitchell tried to play it cool and keep his worries to himself. When Katelyn noted the injury's ghastly appearance (which she frequently did), he told her it was fine. It didn't hurt; it would go away when it felt like it. But secretly, he obsessed. He'd stand before a mirror, turn his head, and look. And look. Red, swollen (at least as large as a marble), tender to the touch, raw, damp. It wanted to bleed and *would* bleed, he found out several times, with any minor application of pressure.

The thing was a distraction. It consumed him, to the point he barely cared about work, and he certainly cared little at all what the hell was going on with Sheriff Palmer's "investigation" of Nathaniel Golding's very obvious suicide. That man's death got him out of a bad divorce case. Hallelujah, whatever.

Palmer stopped by his office one day. Came through the door, sat down in the plastic chair at the front of his desk, and informed Dean that there'd been a gun, a .32 pistol, right next to Golding's body.

"I figured something killed him." Dean rubbed at the wound and stared over Palmer's head.

I just don't care right now, Sheriff. I should see a doctor.

He covered the spot with a bandage and attempted to go about his life. He found the wherewithal to pick up the phone and return Savannah Golding's calls. She cried about Nathaniel and cried about her daughter, because Marion was *gone*, and nobody gave her hope they'd find her. Dean pressed the bandage with one hand and the bridge of his nose with the other and told himself he didn't need anymore fucking problems. Then he told her it would be all right.

He tried to be nice to Katelyn.

He tried to talk to new clients. He tried to research and draft.

But all he could *really* do was fret over the nasty wound from that nasty room in that nasty house.

Constable Riley Saunders called a few days after Sheriff Palmer's visit. This was at least a week and a half after his initial trip to the Evenware house. She asked if he'd heard the news about Nathaniel Golding.

"I don't know."

"Suicide. It was his gun. Meth and pills in his truck."

"I heard. I've read the paper and talked to Savannah."

"Are you okay, Mr. Mitchell?" She sounded like she knew he wasn't.

He lied and told her he was.

And he did the same thing that night, when Katelyn said: "You're still wearing the bandage. And when you're not, you're compulsive about it. Go see a doctor."

He was sitting in the living room trying to read. It wasn't happening.

"It's not getting worse."

"Come on, Dean." She took his book away and sat down next to him. "At some point, if it's not getting better, it's getting worse."

He touched the bandage, just light pressure, and felt a trace of pain. It must have shown on his face, because Katelyn flashed him a knowing frown—a straight-up *I told you so.*

"I really think it's better," he lied. "A few more days."

She stood up and walked away.

Damn her, he thought. Truly. *Go to the doctor. I'm so worried.* But then, upon receiving a response that wasn't exactly what she wanted? Leave. That she was *right* only made it worse—she *knew* he was scared. She had no right to lose her patience with him. If it were *her* with the marble-sized, infected knot on the side of her neck, would she be scared? *When I'm dead, you'll blame me for dying. I've been good to you. You sit at home and play your goddamned guitar because of me.*

He calmed down and thought about looking for her, just to talk, not to yell.

But when he heard her in the kitchen getting something out of the refrigerator, he did not move.

29

UNTIL HE DID.

He went to the half-bath just off the living room and turned on the light and shut the door. He removed the bandage from his neck and turned his head so he could look at the wound. But there was no wound, because there was no reflection. The mirror revealed a frail and monstrous thing covered with hair that was matted in blood.

Then it was gone and was just his reflection, and that glowing red knot on his neck that was neither better nor worse. It glistened and itched, and Dean felt an irrational hatred towards Katelyn, his life, *everything*, boiling up from his stomach.

Indigestion, probably.

He tore off a wad of toilet paper and touched it to the knot. It itched and itched, and to hell with it. He scrubbed as though he might actually erase the thing from his neck.

He scrubbed until his phone—a replacement iPhone, yet another fatality from his night at the Evenware house—alerted him of a text message.

From Savannah Golding. Asking him to come over.

HE REDRESSED THE WOUND AND left without telling Katelyn. It occurred to him as he drove that this was not a good idea. But did it really matter?

He eventually found himself in Savannah Golding's driveway, watching another round of snow flurries, not wanting to go inside, but not wanting to stay out here with nothing but the snow and his thoughts, either.

So he went up to her door and knocked.

She answered, dressed in sweatpants and a tee shirt. No makeup, hair down, swollen eyes. She forced a smile and told him to come inside. She then apologized and told him it was probably a mistake, sorry for asking; there were enough problems without getting him in trouble with Katelyn.

He waved off her concerns and took a seat on the couch.

The house was dark. Only one light was burning, a reading lamp in the corner of the entryway.

"I think I'm suicidal." She sat down next to him.

Dean picked at the bandage on his neck.

"I know she's dead," Savannah said. "She's dead, just like him. Maybe not the same way. Maybe I have no reason for thinking that. But I think so."

"Don't jump to that."

"It's not a jump. He was unbearable, especially before he died. Moody. A bastard. We talked about murder once, do you remember?"

She smiled at the memory.

"You were talking about Marion," Dean said.

"She had to put up with it, just like I did. Do you want a drink?"

He almost said no. Then said yes.

She left the room and returned with two glasses and a bottle of American Honey. She poured them both an inch or so and set the bottle on the table.

"Let's face something, Dean." She lit a cigarette, took a deep drag, and coughed. "Our blood isn't worth a damn."

He just looked at her and sipped his drink.

"Do you think we're good people?" she said.

"We're not the worst."

She sucked down half the cigarette and set it in an ashtray by the whiskey bottle. "I just want my Marion. Asshole's brains can stay where they are."

"Of course."

"How many times can you call your wife a whore bitch before you realize it's you and take yourself out? And Marion just stayed at that damned job. She'd walk some of those trails just to not come home." Suddenly, she was studying him intently. "What is wrong with your neck?"

It was going to happen eventually, he thought, and removed the bandage.

She leaned in. "That looks bad. What is it?"

"I hurt myself when I went looking for your husband. A splinter or a nail or something."

"That was almost two weeks ago."

"I know. It's not healing, and I'm obsessed with it. I make it worse."

She crushed out the cigarette and left the room. She returned with cotton balls, hydrogen peroxide, antibiotic ointment, and a clean bandage. She dabbed the raw area atop the knot with peroxide, then put antibiotic ointment on a clean bandage and applied it as snugly as possible.

Savannah Golding was looking at him again. She looked so damned old, Dean thought. Sixty, at least, instead of forty-nine or fifty or whatever she actually was. He'd never seen her like this.

But she was also beautiful.

In a tragic sort of way.

5

ON FEBRUARY 8, ALMOST A month after the discovery of Nathaniel Golding's body, Riley Saunders found herself sitting in her Jeep outside the Harrelston Ridge Ranger Station, three miles north of town on the left side of the highway. Harrelston Ridge was a steep, thousand-foot-tall oblong mountain east of town that offered breathtaking views of the "Arkansas Grand Canyon"—miles and miles of mountains, ridges, bluffs, and valleys. The ridge was the namesake feature of their district of Ozark National Forest, and the ranger station in Ellingwood, built in 1999, was the newest in the network.

Riley had just gotten off the phone with Sheriff Palmer.

Yes, they'd been looking for the girl—Marion. No reason to think she was anywhere but very far away, away from her god-awful, dramatic, immoral, alcoholic,

34

and apparently suicidal parents. Yes, he'd already talked to the old black guy at the ranger station—Robert—talked to him himself. Helpful but not *super* helpful. Finally: *Relax, Constable. She'll turn up somewhere over the summer and we'll learn she was down in Guadalajara enjoying the freedoms that come with being young and healthy and tied down to absolutely nothing.*

Riley didn't buy it. Dad blows his brains out at about the same time Daughter disappears—to Riley Saunders, this didn't seem like a *trip to Mexico* fact pattern.

Robert was in the station, sitting on his stool behind the counter. This was his perch for three days a week, from nine till closing. He flashed her a warm, toothy smile as she entered.

"I'm glad to see you, Constable," he said. "I assume you're here to talk about Marion Golding?"

"That's right."

"I remember talking to you before. You were thinking it wasn't so innocent."

"That's still what I think."

"I agree with you."

"I don't have any theories," Riley said, "just the faint working idea that there is a link between her dad's suicide and her disappearance. I'm not alone, but Palmer's under the impression he's put in his due diligence and can just wait for a postcard from Mexico. Maybe he's right."

"I'm glad you came in here. I've been thinking." He held up a *just one minute* index finger, knelt below the counter, and emerged with a topographic map of the Harrelston Ridge District. "She didn't have a car. She

35

walked or jogged to work every morning, no matter the weather." He pointed to a line on the map, traced a pudgy finger along it. "Now, I told you all about the Oak Falls Trail. Starts here behind the building and goes north along the creek for about two miles till it gets to the falls. She loved that trail."

"We hiked it," Riley said.

Savannah Golding had alluded to this, too; she'd mentioned the girl hitting the trails instead of coming home in the evenings.

"As did I, despite my poor old knees. I think we all hiked it multiple times." He waved a finger over the array of swirling lines that covered the map. "But what about all these?"

Palmer, Riley knew, claimed his men had "beaten the bushes for days." No doubt they'd hit some of these trails. But as far as anybody knew, Marion had never shown an interest in serious hiking or backpacking, and she had no feasible way to reach many of the trailheads, as she didn't have a vehicle. She'd taken to wandering the Oak Falls Trail because it was *right here* and trekking it till dark beat the hell out of going home to her drunken mother. Beyond that? Riley found it hard to believe the girl had wandered all the way, say, to the top of Harrelston Ridge. And even if she had…

"Which ones aren't accessible from here without lengthy drives?" Riley said. "As in, there's no feasible way for her to even get to them?"

"I've got the list, Constable." He reached under the counter again and withdrew a sheet of paper covered in his jagged yet neat handwriting. "I've got three lists on here. Right here are the trails I just don't think she could've made it to. Now, she's been gone so long, she could be in Oklahoma or Missouri by now. But if we're assuming she never meant to go very far, don't bother with these." He pointed at several of them on the map, then moved on to the next list. "These are maybe within her reach, maybe not, depending on how good her legs are. I listed these trails because they're very popular, every season. You don't get privacy on'em. Even this time of year, there'll be hikers on them." And finally, the third list. "Right here are the ones I think we need to make sure we search. All within five miles of here, and you don't have to scale up or down any mountainsides or climb rock faces to get to them."

Riley pulled the paper across the counter. Five trails. He'd narrowed dozens down to five.

Robert made his way down the list; his knowledge, Riley thought, was impressive: "The Deer Run Trail is about two miles from here. She could follow the highway for less than half an hour and hit the trailhead. The Ozark Trail intersects Deer Run about four miles off the road. Goes west all the way through the Boston Mountains to the Oklahoma border. Popular with backpackers. Wouldn't hurt to spend a few hours out there. This old trail here, 9501, is an old forest road, goes up to Tenmile Point. I doubt she'd give a hoot about it, but you can't ever tell. The Harrelston Lookout trail should be more popular than it is. Starts right on the edge of town. You can hit it at the end of Spruce Street. Goes four miles to a lookout about halfway up Harrelston Ridge. Last one here is the Roundtop Mountain bypass trail. Take the Ozark Trail east and make a left. Beautiful path, clear trail. That said, hardly anybody knows about it, and it's pretty much empty this time of year."

"You know your stuff."

"I've spent days making these lists. I can't help you with all the trails, Constable. My knees won't let me tackle Harrelston Lookout or Tenmile Point. No ma'am. But the others? Let's get started."

RILEY CALLED SHERIFF PALMER AND confirmed that the Deer Run Trail had already been searched in its entirety, probably more than once, and over twelve miles of the Ozark Trail had been followed, too; no, he wasn't sure if anybody had gone up the intersecting Roundtop Mountain bypass. Thus, of the trails Robert had listed, only the last three needed to be searched.

"I'll leave the two steep ones to you, Constable, if you don't mind," he said. "I can drive on up to the other side of Roundtop Mountain and hit the trail from its other end, instead of having to hike all the way out to the Ozark Trail. It'll take me the rest of the day. Should be cell service out there."

"How long is it?" Riley said.

"Five, six miles one way. Level terrain."

"You're sure you're up for it?"

"No, ma'am. But I'll do what I can. I won't kill myself. Promise."

They swapped phone numbers, and Riley left to go attempt the first of her challenges, the Harrelston Lookout Trail. Between this and the old forest road, she imagined the lookout was more likely to draw Marion's eye.

Riley went home and changed into a pair of nylon hiking pants and a breathable Under Armor shirt. She looped a ponytail through the back of a black baseball cap adorned with the constable star and grabbed a Gatorade from the refrigerator.

Then she drove to the end of Spruce Street, parked on the edge of the field just off the cul-de-sac, and started toward a trail that began at the end of the street. The trail was marked with a small wooden sign; it set off in a straight line toward the heavily wooded wall that was Harrleston Ridge. The first two miles were level; the trail meandered in and out of the woods and passed by a stagnant pond. She walked slowly, scanning both sides of the trail as best she could, stopping every ten or twenty feet to look around.

The last two miles, beginning at a log bridge that crossed the bayou, were much steeper, the last half mile being a perpetual uphill trudge, switchback after switchback as the trail climbed the steep east slopes of Harrelston Ridge.

The trail faded out at a rocky bluff just a little over halfway up.

Riley took a seat on the bluff and allowed herself a generous gulp of Gatorade. She felt good, though she'd found nothing.

She'd made it all the way up here and had uncovered no sign whatsoever of recent human activity anywhere along the trail.

6

DEAN MITCHELL EMERGED FROM THE Cove County Courthouse in Harrison at a quarter after eleven that morning, proceeded wearily to his truck, and collapsed into the driver's seat. He could not blame his exhaustion on the hearing. That had been standard child support bullshit: sit at a table, provide a pinhead with a few half-baked reasons why his client was a forgetful but hard working piece of shit, get a new date, get out. The hearing had been nothing at all. It was the *weight* of recent history bringing him down, especially the last two weeks, since the night he'd gone to Savannah's.

He hadn't seen her since, thank God. Lord knows what he'd say to her.

There was enough stress in his life without her luring him over there and wooing him and making things a thousand times worse. Was it fair to say that Katelyn was responsible for sixty percent of his problems? If so, Savannah Golding was the other forty percent. Self-indulgent, irresponsible bullshit, of course. Katelyn's self-pity and dramatics were suffocating; Savannah Golding was at best a guilty pleasure. These two women were not responsible for all his problems. Nevertheless, he figured it didn't hurt to lay some blame where it was due.

And oh God, he was tired.

One no-stress hearing, and look at him! Slumped in his truck seat, head thrown back, breathing like he'd just jogged an eight-minute mile (not that he could do *that* nowadays), and feeling the beginnings of a new and perhaps concerning pounding behind his eyes. A casual observer wouldn't rule out a mental breakdown or heart attack.

I have to get it together.

It was time, damn it, to make *sure* everything was okay, and if not, then get it that way. Or just die. Those were his options. And by *everything* being *okay*, he was primarily concerned with his physical well-being. Everything else, he felt sure, would fall into place if he could just get a (knowledgeable) confirmation that he wasn't being eaten alive by cancer or staph.

His relationship with Katelyn would improve. He'd go to the doctor, come home, speak aloud the good news, and Katelyn would sarcastically congratulate him on doing what he should've done two weeks ago; then, eventually, they'd have their first meaningful (civil) conversation since the pre-Evenware days. Long term, maybe their marriage would work, maybe it wouldn't. But the status quo of the last few weeks was unsustainable. That creepy and not-so-joking flirtation

41

with killing her he'd shared with Savannah would boil up, come to life, and end Katelyn's goddamned pity party for *good.*

And Savannah. After his doctor visit, he'd call her up and deliver the good news about his neck. An infection caused a nearby lymph node to swell. A round of antibiotics would fix the whole thing. The red marble below his ear would be gone in a week. He could already hear her congratulations (and they'd sound much sweeter than his wife's, no doubt). And he'd say something like, "Look, I feel bad about Nathaniel. And Marion. I want to help. But coming over there the other night wasn't a good idea. It messed me up even more than I already was. We can't be doing that, okay? At least until I'm done with Katelyn, and who knows about that. Any word about Marion?"

Yes, things would calm down.

But he did not have the mental fortitude to address either of his problematic females until he addressed himself.

When he was able, he sat up in the driver's seat, started the truck, and headed south. There was a walk-in clinic on the way into Harrison. He'd been in there before. But after he pulled in and parked, he did not get out. He thought at first he was merely hesitating, but as it turned out, he *never* opened the door. Because he was scared, no *terrified*, of what would show up in a medical examination. He was fleeing something that was beyond even his imagination. Cancer, staph… He'd heard of those. He'd probably live through either, or both, at least for a good while. Honestly, he was scared it was something worse.

42

This realization almost made him laugh.

What the *hell* could that thing on his neck be that was worse than a cancerous tumor or a raging infection? *It doesn't matter. I don't need to be here. Antibiotics probably won't work, and I don't need any lectures about stress and high blood pressure.*

Forget the doctor. For now at least.

He pulled back out on the highway and started again toward Ellingwood.

As he drove, he scrolled through the numbers on his phone until he came to Mary Evenware's.

He dialed it, and Lewis, of course, was the one to answer.

"It's Dean Mitchell. How are you?"

Lewis said he was fine.

"How is Mary doing today?"

"Not well, Mr. Mitchell. I'm sitting here with her now, but she hasn't said much today." His voice lowered some. "It's actually been very bad. Just a few months ago, she was normal, and now... more often than not, I wouldn't promise you she knows who she is."

This was the most Dean had ever heard the man speak, a clear indication that Lewis was distraught about his mother's condition.

Perfectly understandable, but it caused Dean to question how he should handle the rest of this call.

"I wanted to ask about our last meeting," Dean said, "maybe go from there."

A long pause.

"Okay," Lewis said.

"If Mary is able to talk, I'd love to talk to her."

"I'll use the speaker, but don't count on much."

Dean took a moment to gather himself. "When I was there last, Mary said something about how she's got someone out there taking care of the old house. And she told me she doesn't think I should go out there."

Silence.

Until Lewis said, "Yes?"

"Why does she want it 'taken care of'—as in, torn down?"

Dean imagined Lewis studying his mother, trying to determine how well she was comprehending this and what he should say in front of her.

"She sees it as a hazard, Mr. Mitchell. She's never wanted me out there. It's been sitting empty and it's falling down, anyway."

"And she hired Nathaniel Golding to take it down."

"He was a local handyman. I'm sure you know that. When she decided she wanted it down, she hired him. This was last November. Better than burning it down, which I heard her talk about, even before she got bad. I asked her to let me do it. She was adamant in her *no*."

"She told me I shouldn't go out there, too. But I did, and we all know what I found."

"Yes. Nathaniel Golding committed suicide."

"And I've gotten very sick."

More silence.

"Sick?" Lewis said.

"I cut myself. It's a bad wound, and it's still not healed."

"She told you not to go out there, didn't she?"

Congratulations, jackass, Dean Mitchell thought.

"I just think it's *odd*," Dean said, "and I'm not trying to say or suggest anything here. But I think it's very *odd* that after twenty or thirty years or however long of that place sitting out there falling into the ground, she decided it was time to tear it down. Then, right after she wakes up just long enough to tell me not to go out there, well, I find Nathaniel Golding and get an infectious tumor on my neck. And if you *really* want to get conspiratorial, feel free to note the fact that Marion Golding has been gone since about the time her dad shot himself in your mother's demolition project. I hoped you might have something to tell me. But if you're going to be a smartass, whatever."

He ended the call and pulled over and studied himself in the rearview mirror.

What in the world had brought *that* on?

Exhaustion. That's what it was.

He was easing back onto the highway again when he received a text from Lewis: *Come by the house.*

LEWIS LET HIM INTO THE dining room and offered him a beer. Dean accepted.

"She's asleep upstairs." Lewis set two Blue Moons on the table and took a seat across from him. "I'll tell you what I know, and it isn't much. Sorry for the snide remark."

Dean shrugged.

Lewis said: "Last year, Mom was fine. She was as active and *aware* as you can expect an old woman to be. She'd read books, talk my ears off. I remember Halloween. Her at the door, greeting the kids. But it

45

started happening in November. She would have little episodes where she'd talk to herself or slip away, but Thanksgiving was the first time I caught her just sitting and staring and I was shouting to get her attention, and she didn't know where she was when I had it. And do you know what happened between Halloween and Thanksgiving, Mr. Mitchell?"

"The house."

"Yes. She went out to the old house. Walked. You know it's several miles out into the woods to get there. Not only did she *walk all the way out there*, Mr. Mitchell, she went after dark. I know the exact date, because it was the November full moon. The fourteenth. She's actually done this before. Not annually, nothing like that, but she goes down there sometimes, at night, during full moons. She's always told me she has bad dreams and checking on it gives her peace of mind. This time, she was down there for a long time, and she wouldn't talk about it. That's not like her. She said she was tired and was going to bed. I sat by her most of the night. I heard her say, 'The berries, the berries.' And that was all. That's all she said, all night.

"The next day is when she said she wanted it down. She talked to me about it. We had lunch. She acted normal again, which made me happy. She said she wanted the old house torn down. Why? 'That house doesn't contain a single good memory,' she said. So I told her okay, I'll go out there with some lighter fluid and a lighter. She told me absolutely not. 'The woods are thick, you fool. No need in burning down the mountainside. I want as little advertisement as possible. And I don't want you out there at all.'

"The guy she hired, Nathaniel, came up here right after Christmas. She took him into her room and shut the door. They were quiet till he started shouting. She stared at the walls for two days after that.

"I don't know what to think about it. I just know there's something there she doesn't like, and she wants it gone. Or she did. When she still had her mind."

7

THE NEXT EVENING, RILEY SAUNDERS stood quietly in the remains of the Evenware House. She'd been out here most of the day, telling herself (repeatedly) that she'd leave by sunset.

But the sun was setting, and here she was, still standing in the room where Nathaniel Golding had shot himself.

She was looking for the bullet. Because it hadn't been in his head, and it was *still* nowhere to be found. The missing bullet had been written off as an anomaly. The man had obviously shot himself, so what did it matter? For all anybody knew, it could have ricocheted off an old nail and flown out the broken window into the night!

Theoretically.

Riley didn't totally buy it.

And thanks to what she'd found this morning, her imagination was raging.

AT ELEVEN A.M., RILEY KNOCKED on Savannah Golding's front door. She was not in uniform. The appearance of a law enforcement officer, she'd long ago decided, put some people off, even when it was the local constable who never bothered a soul.

Savannah Golding opened the door, not quite looking like hell. She was dressed, her hair was up, her eyes were clear.

"I'm glad to see you, Constable," she said. "Are you here to talk about my daughter?"

"And husband, if you don't mind."

"I swear, you're the first. Come in."

Savannah led her to a seat in the den and offered her coffee or tea, perhaps even lunch, all of which Riley declined.

The den was gray and quiet and smelled like smoke. There was a partially-complete jigsaw puzzle on the coffee table. An ocean scene, complete with sunset and lighthouse.

"I'm looking for anything that's got orange on top and water at the bottom." Savannah took a seat next to Riley and feigned interest in her current project. "The transition between the ocean and sky is just driving me crazy."

Riley decided to ignore—as politely as possible—the woman's invitation to comb through the puzzle pieces. She also chose to skip past idle chitchat about the weather—*warming up, maybe the snow is done for the year?*

49

She got straight to the point: "You said I'm the first. What did you mean?"

"They act like they're totally separate things, Nathaniel and Marion. Can't possibly be related, even though they're literally related! When they found Nathaniel, I talked to everybody, or I felt like I talked to everybody. But when I called about Marion...? It was too quiet. I *think* I remember the sheriff or somebody bringing up how her disappearance kind of coincided with what Nathaniel did. It's not like they ignored it. But Nathaniel shot himself. They searched the whole area, and she was nowhere around. So no connection, they said. I don't know." She'd been looking at the puzzle. Now she looked up. "I'm glad you're here."

"I don't have anything new. I've been looking for her, and I think there's a connection between her and your husband's suicide." Riley removed a small notepad from her back pocket and flipped it open to a certain page. She handed it to Savannah. "I talked to Robert again. In his opinion, those are the trails Marion could have feasibly been on after she left work Thursday evening. We've looked at all of them, and there's no sign of her. You said she enjoyed 'wandering,' and Robert said the same thing. Did you ever hear of anywhere else she enjoyed walking or hiking? Did she mention any places she'd like to try?"

"Not that I know of."

"She never said anything about the Evenware property?"

Savannah shook her head. "Never a word."

"And based on everything you've heard, your husband was out there...?"

"He got contacted last November, by Mary Evenware. He was being semi-civil to me back then. He was drinking too much. Drugs, too, but he was civil. So he came home from meeting with her and told me she was going to pay him a lot of money—I think it was five thousand dollars—to take it down. Like we discussed when he died, Constable, he started in early December. And I guess he went out there and shot himself sometime around…"

"He was found on the sixteenth of January," Riley said, "and he'd been dead a few days. Did he ever talk about the Evenware property in front of Marion?"

"I would say, after about the new year, I never saw him, and I don't think Marion did, either. I—we—might have seen him once or twice. It's possible she heard him talking about the old house, especially before the new year."

"How was their relationship?"

"Nathaniel and Marion's? When she was little, it was okay. But when she got to be a teenager, not so good. You know how it is, Constable. Teenage girl."

"Was Marion the type to run away?"

Savannah stared hard at the puzzle. Shifted a piece or two around. "For a couple of days maybe. That's why I wasn't alarmed. I thought maybe she'd hit a trail she read about and hiked into another town. Nothing, you know, long term. She isn't that independent. She doesn't have a car. Not a lot of money. And do you know what? She loves me. She doesn't always like to be around me. But I don't think she'd just leave. Surely she wouldn't leave without saying something first."

"You said Nathaniel might have come around once or twice after New Year's Day."

"Maybe."

"You don't remember?"

"I saw him a time or two. He'd come in and act like he hadn't been gone for days at a time. Shower. Eat something. A time or two."

This, Riley thought, *could be* an unturned rock.

"He came back here? In January? You can say that with confidence?"

She hoped she wasn't pressing Savannah too hard.

But Savannah was taking it well. She surely knew Riley wasn't here to interrogate her. Only to help.

"Yeah, he definitely did. At least once. Maybe twice."

"I know you said he acted like nothing was going on, but if you *had* to say that he did something unusual during one of these home visits, what would it be? What was the most unusual thing he did?"

Savannah squinted her eyes for a bit as if she found the question unintelligible. She mindlessly put a hand out and ran a few fingers through the puzzle pieces.

"Most unusual thing… Well, one time he did get on the computer. He doesn't like computers much. He has—had—an email he checked sometimes. I guess it had slipped my mind." She closed her eyes. "I guess it would've been after the first. I remember it being fresh on my mind that we hadn't seen him over the holidays, but now, here he was. He came in and showered and ate something and got on the computer. Left again."

"Has anybody looked at the computer?" Riley had certainly never done it.

"Nobody. Palmer looked around, but he didn't ask to get on the computer. Doubt you'd find anything, anyway, Constable. I'm telling you, Nathaniel was almost illiterate when it comes to technology, and I don't care about it. Even Marion. She's got her phone. She never used the computer."

"Do you mind?"

Savannah shook her head and shooed her toward the back of the house. The spare bedroom across the hall from Marion's room was a storage area and makeshift office. Two walls were stacked with various grades of junk. The closet was overflowing with clothes. Dusty exercise equipment was crammed into one corner. And in front of the window was a rolling desk, atop which was a Dell desktop that, Riley discovered, was one click of the keyboard away from springing to life.

Riley perused the machine's contents. The files on the hard drive seemed completely innocent: school assignments, photos that had probably been uploaded from a cell phone years ago, a few dozen songs in an ancient version of iTunes.

The history of the Dell's only web browser was similarly thin: a few trips to Amazon and MSN... email... Facebook... These were from several weeks ago. But on January 2, there had been a Google search and a trip to a website that stood out amongst what little history the browser had: KYLER CUSTOM WEAPONRY.

She clicked around on the site and made a note about it in her phone, then searched the room she was in and went down the hall to the master bedroom.

53

Messy. Partially consumed drinks and food were stacked beside the bed. The smell of smoke was thick.

She opened a few drawers in the dresser. Nothing of interest. Peered under the bed. Dusty darkness. She opened the closet. Clothes. Shoes beneath them. Perfectly normal. And she didn't know what she was looking for, if anything, but a small box on the shelf above the clothes caught her eye. It was roughly twice the size of a ring box, red, with black letters etched on the top and sides: KYLER CUSTOM WEAPONRY.

Riley pulled the top off the box, revealing a bed of foam with three indentions cut into it. Two were filled. A bullet in each. The other slot was empty. Riley lifted one of the cartridges out of the foam, a shiny silver-colored bullet in what she assumed was a nickel-coated brass case. She held it up in front of her eyes, rotated it a bit, and wondered if this was what she thought it was.

The writing inside the lid confirmed it: .32 ammunition, solid silver, nickel-plated brass casing.

RILEY WONDERED: WHY WOULD HE purchase silver bullets? Were they *real*? What were silver bullets used for? Did this say something about why Nathaniel killed himself? And of course, had he used the missing bullet in his suicide? Savannah claimed to know nothing about it.

"I don't know, Constable. I just know he was crazy."

Riley studied the Kyler website. Yes, their bullets were real ammunition and were fireable (though some of the customer reviews, Riley noted, mentioned the bullets causing jams). They were *real* silver bullets, through Kyler's site stated they were primarily sold as novelty items. A Google search accomplished nothing but reminding Riley of all the classic lore surrounding silver bullets.

A narrative was forming in her mind. Not one she'd share with anybody. Because if it wasn't crazy, it was at least close to it. He shot himself in the head with a silver bullet because... Because he was ill. Because he'd killed his daughter and couldn't stand it.

The *silver bullet* suggested he thought himself a (literal) monster. This aspect of her narrative was insane enough to make her pause. As was the pesky fact that she actually had no idea *what* bullet he'd shot himself with.

For all Riley knew, those bullets were a joke, or...

No. In the weeks before he died, Nathaniel Golding was estranged from his wife, on bad terms with his daughter, and in the midst of a job that was not going well—he'd not come close to bringing down the Evenware House. No, he'd not purchased a *joke*.

The silver bullet was probably what had gone through his head and killed him. And like his daughter, it was missing.

She'd scoured the upstairs room, searched every corner, crack, and crevice. No bullet, silver or otherwise, nor any sign of one.

The palm-sized .32 that had done the job was a "mouse gun" at best, but at suicide range, the round had apparently experienced few difficulties blasting its way through his brain and out the other side of his skull.

"Not a bit of doubt what happened," Randall Jennings, the county coroner, had said. "The wound was right there, clear as day, just in front of his right ear. Exit wound a little higher up on the other side of the head. Nothing grotesque. The mouse gun ain't gonna blow your skull open like in the movies."

"Palmer said they didn't find the bullet."

"Well it ain't in his head."

Could it have exited Nathaniel Golding's head with enough force to blow through a wall? Riley now thought, standing in the middle of the suicide room. *Likely* not, according to Jennings. The bullet was probably lodged in a wall somewhere, though Riley was beginning to doubt this; the room had been combed over multiple times.

She told herself she'd return sometime with a ladder and a better light than the one on her phone.

The front door opened.

Heavy footsteps downstairs.

Riley put her left hand on her gun and quietly stepped out of the room and returned to the stairs. She'd killed her phone light, and the sunset was fading to twilight. The house was dim, almost dark.

The footsteps stopped. But where? She could not gather *where* her guest might be.

Near the plant growing in the corner?

She descended one step.

And the answer to her question appeared below her. Dean Mitchel stepped into a faint glimmer of light at the base of the stairs. He was dressed haphazardly in sweatpants and a leather jacket. He looked ill, and he was staring up at her. His eyes were wide and blank, lips slightly separated, as if he might have something to say but wasn't quite sure.

"Mr. Mitchell?" Riley finally said.

To which the lawyer turned around and took off out the front door, into the cold and fading twilight.

RILEY KNOCKED AT LEAST A dozen times on the Mitchells' front door before accepting that nobody was going to answer. But there *was* somebody home; there were multiple lights on, and Katelyn's Honda was in the driveway.

This is why Riley tried the knob. And when the door did not open, she went into the garage and tried that door. It was unlocked. She entered, announcing her presence as she crossed the threshold.

She passed through a dark laundry room into a short corridor that connected to a half bath to the right and the kitchen to the left.

Cigarette smoke. Unsettling, since she'd never seen either of the Mitchells smoking.

She turned left and entered the kitchen.

Katelyn was sitting at a breakfast table, staring down at a cigarette that was burning between the index and middle fingers of her left hand. She was using a saucer as an ashtray.

She looks terrible, Riley thought, *and it's not just the cigarette and the way she's staring at it.* No, Katelyn's face was glossy and colorless, except for the puffy redness beneath her right eye.

"Mrs. Mitchell?" Riley did not approach the table. "I'm sorry to just come in. The door was unlocked."

57

Katelyn looked up and dropped the cigarette in the saucer. "He went out."

"Dean?"

"That's him."

She coughed. It was broken and violent. She shoved the saucer away.

"I just saw him," Riley said.

"Dead?"

"He acted strangely."

Katelyn pulled the saucer back toward her. "That's too bad."

8

KATELYN REGRETTED SMOKING THE CIGARETTE. It had a more detrimental effect on her than downing a bottle of whiskey would have. Or, that's what she blamed the long, miserable night on. *Something* caused her to spend most of the night on the side of the bed, one hand on her stomach, the other clutching the nightstand, as if she were on the brink of falling into the floor.

Last night had been a marathon. Sleepless, sick stomach, burning lungs, the perfect ode to a wrecked marriage.

Whatever. It was nine a.m. The house was full of sunshine, the day was cold but beautiful, and she could look back at last night (and her marriage) and say, yes, with certainty, that it was over, thank God, and she'd take things from here.

What to do?

Nashville is what she came up with. Go east. Get out of the Ozarks, get out of the state, get far away from Ellingwood and Dean Mitchell. Would she actually make a real *go* at songwriting, like she'd always wanted to do? Did she have a real shot at it?

It didn't matter. She'd always wanted to go there, immerse herself in an environment that stimulated and encouraged her. Ellingwood was a nice little place, but it was nothing, the same nothing, every single day, with the same depressing husband whose only care was trying to be Mr. Big in a tiny map dot that barely qualified as a wide spot in the road.

So, Nashville, *if* she'd actually do it.

Was she mad enough and hurt enough, after Dean's… abuse? That, she thought, was the culmination of everything, the signal that it was okay to say to hell with it. It had to be more than anger. Anger was shallow and evaporated quickly. If she left, it was because of a more substantial, deeply rooted problem. If this problem were real, she thought she could do it. If not, she'd end up feeling like a fool. She'd load up the Honda and make it fifty miles down the road, realize this was an overreaction to her husband being a stressed, sick, and drunken asshole, and she'd come back to help. She would not abandon a marriage, no matter how bleak its outlook, if anything worth salvaging was salvageable.

What about last night? The crying, the heartburn, the trips to the toilet, the welt beneath her eye. What about *beyond* last night? The lack of communication. The fundamental differences on life. The welt beneath her eye. The fact that she truly, in some ways, hated him.

The certainty that he did not love her. The welt beneath her eye.

Nashville had to happen. In terms she'd never put in a song: *Fuck this shit*.

She spent the first half of the day sorting and packing and loading her things into her car. *Her* car. Dean had been nothing but (poor) support during the seven exhausting hours she spent at a Memphis dealership purchasing *her* Honda, using money *she* had been saving for years as a down payment.

A suitcase full of clothes and toiletries went in first. Then a collection of novels and her notebook. This was the easy stuff. The hardest part was the two hour period she spent sorting through pictures and sentimental. Dreadful. She came close to crying when she came upon a 5x7 of Dean and her father together at a Cowboys game, both smiling and healthy and enjoying life. Now, almost ten years later, the older man was dead and the good-looking fellow on the right…? He'd abandoned her long ago, and now he was—she was certain—sick and crazy and not getting better.

She was exhausted after a few hours of sorting, packing, and loading, so exhausted that she felt her desire to get in the car and drive away evaporating.

She collapsed on the living room sofa and found herself in a half-awake state wondering where her husband was and if she should care. Finally, she fell asleep. She awoke (a little) and spent a blurry period looking at Nashville on her phone. Places to live, places to eat, places to work, because she'd need a "real" job, until she could pay her bills by scribbling lyrics and strumming her guitar. All these thoughts and more. Looking at her phone. Wondering what she was doing.

When she at last got up, the light through the vertical window by the front door had faded to a dull gray. Snow flurries were flying, barely visible in the orange light of a nearby street lamp. What a snowy winter this was, even by Ozark standards.

The horror returned. A reenactment out there in the snow of a scene that had taken place in her studio, and she saw the guitars out there, too, faint holograms, hanging from tree limbs like fruit; in the midst of the snow and guitars, two figures, screaming silently, and then, one retreating, one swinging, not much of a swing, as if it had realized something, but a swing nonetheless, and a swing that connected.

God, or something like God, turned off the television. *I show you this, and you know why.* No. She couldn't stay here. The ghosts were settling in, and they'd only multiply and strengthen.

My guitars.

Had she nearly forgotten the most obvious thing? Or things? She wasn't going anywhere without—at the very least—her two favorite guitars. Two was the maximum her vehicle could hold, anyway. Dean Mitchell, Esquire, could sell off the rest and use the proceeds to treat his godforsaken neck wound. She didn't care.

She started up the stairs… and stopped when she realized her heart was racing out of control for no reason at all. She was not exerting herself. She was not frightened… was she?

She put a hand atop her left breast and felt her heart's rapid fire pounding. Cold sweat broke over her brow. A panic attack? This was not a problem to which she was accustomed. And why? Why would she be panicked?

He's upstairs.

She was certain of this, just as she was certain that he was still angry. Last night's Angry Lawyer was back this evening for round two.

No reason to think this. She hadn't been upstairs all day. He *could* be up there, but how would she know? Probably she was just fretting over the idea of *actually leaving.* Yes, that was it, and right on cue, upon realizing that, her heart rate slowed. She removed her hand from her chest, took one more step up, and felt herself smile. Truly, everything was okay. Get the guitars and—

Something crashed below her—*the front door flew open*, she thought, and the blast of Arctic air that immediately followed the racket confirmed it.

Panic returned as she tried to convince herself that the wind had blown open the door. Maybe it hadn't been latched? Except it *had* been latched. She'd just been down there looking at ghosts and snow flurries and there hadn't been nearly enough wind to make such a violent entrance.

"Dean?"

She dared a step down. She had to go somewhere, and there was nowhere to go upstairs, nothing to serve as a weapon, except a guitar... which, now that she thought about it, a guitar wouldn't be half bad, and there was the octagon window, too...

No. She stepped down, because it was probably a whole bunch of nothing, or it was her husband, and despite her prior thoughts, as bad as he'd been lately, Dean Mitchell was not a murderous psychopath.

Just this one step down revealed most of the front door, and it was, indeed, standing open. She could also see the ragged, doorknob-sized hole in the wall behind it, because Dean had once laughed in her face when she'd suggested installing a doorstop. Certainly, there was nothing funny about any of this. The front door had just crashed inward, and there was no indication of why or how.

She took another step down and barely heard herself say Dean's name again. Another step, then another, becoming more and more convinced that, while none of this was normal or expected, this was *not* a horror movie. It was okay to go downstairs and close the damned door.

Or so she thought.

Three steps from the bottom, she could see out into the night, and she knew it *wasn't* okay.

There was a figure, more or less human yet somehow *not* human, standing out in the snow-dusted lawn, just beyond the reach of the street lamp. Thin, arms too long. Eyes barely visible and somehow familiar, though they were nothing more than tiny beads of yellow.

She almost said her husband's name again. Her tongue was on the roof of her mouth right behind her front teeth, ready for that one syllable, when the figure retreated into the darkness like a shadow vanishing into a slow growth of light.

Katelyn leapt over the bottom three steps and ran to the door. For a split second she tried to see it, and then reason returned, and she shut the door. Both the latch and deadbolt, upon crashing inward, had obliterated a sizable portion of the wall and door trim, and the door would neither latch nor lock.

The thing out in the yard had done this. What else?

She dragged an antique sewing table—used nowadays to collect keys and coins—in front of the door to hold it shut.

Do we have a gun? she thought. *Anything?*

"I couldn't use it if we did."

A second after she said it, she knew it was untrue. There was a gun in the house, a single-shot .22 that Dean had inherited from his dad, and one night, years ago, before they went to bed, he'd demonstrated how to load, cock, and fire the fifty or sixty-year-old gun. Not much, he'd said. But almost better than nothing.

It was under their bed, or it should be, and maybe she needed to go dig it out and see if she could find the box of .22 shorts he'd bought for it.

Yes, that was a reasonable thing to do.

But first, call somebody.

Constable Riley Saunders had been here last night, hadn't she? Katelyn barely remembered it—she'd been out of her mind—but Riley was a kind, reasonable woman, and she *was* the only law enforcement in this wide spot. Better Riley than 911.

They'd never believe her, not if she told them everything. They'd condescend to her and waste her time and ultimately do nothing. So, Constable Saunders it was.

First the phone.
Then the gun.

9

RILEY ARRIVED AT KATELYN'S HOUSE less than five minutes after Katelyn called her. She pushed through the front door—nudging some sort of small table out of the way—into the living area. The carpet directly in front of the door was strewn with shards of wood from the frame and trim.

Katelyn was sitting in the kitchen, her hands wrapped tightly around a can of Sprite.

Riley pulled up a chair on the opposite side of the table and asked if she was all right.

"I'm breathing," Katelyn said.

"Was he here?"

"I think he was."

Katelyn attempted to explain, but her narrative explained very little. The door. The figure in the yard, which she described as "like a person, but animal-like." *Never mind how this sounds*, Riley thought. Who was this figure? Dean Mitchell? How had he knocked the door in with such force? And why? Nothing was explained.

Riley told herself to breathe deeply, relax, and consider what she'd been told.

"You're quiet," Katelyn said. "I feel like you know something."

"I wish I did."

"But you're thinking something."

The most logical explanation, Riley thought, usually *was* the explanation, which meant Mr. Mitchell had shown up at his house and knocked the door in. Considering the mark on Katelyn's face and how Riley had found her the night before, this was a sane explanation.

But then, if this sane explanation were true, there were flaws with Katelyn's story.

"I'm thinking that I'm confused," Riley said. "The door confuses me. You heard one crash."

"One."

"So the door got knocked in like that with one blow. How does that happen?"

"I don't know."

"If we assume it was Dean—"

"Dean doesn't look like that."

"You said you thought it was Dean."

"I know. I'm just saying, he doesn't look like that."

"Okay. Anybody. Who can do that to a door that's dead bolted, without a lot of kicking or something? Even a sledge hammer wouldn't blow the door in with one hit."

"I don't know. Do you see why I called *you* and not *them*? I don't know."

Riley returned to the front door.

She knelt down and examined the splinters on the floor. The striker plate was amongst the rubble. Someone or something, yes, had knocked the door in… but not in one hit. That simply didn't make sense. Katelyn was mistaken.

She turned her attention to the door, pulled it back toward her, and froze, and not because of the chill of the outside air. But because of the deep gashes that had been slashed across the door's exterior. There were four of these marks, the two middle ones being the deepest and most conspicuous.

Riley hadn't noticed these markings when she arrived. It was dark and she'd been in a hurry to check on Katelyn; once inside, she'd rushed right past the door.

What in the world *was* this? Her imagination was running wild with images that were both frightening and comically impossible. She figured it best not to think of *any* of it right now. Take it for what it was, search for the most obvious and most reasonable explanation. That's what she needed to do.

"What is it?"

Katelyn had at some point stepped out of the kitchen and was standing behind the sofa. She was wrapped in her own arms, and her pathetic appearance was so incredibly authentic that Riley discarded any remaining doubts she had about the woman's sincerity.

And then, there were the marks on the door.

These certainly added to Katelyn's credibility.

"Have you seen these?" Riley stepped out of the way.

Katelyn came around the couch and shook her head.

With her phone, Riley took pictures of the door, the destroyed frame, and the mess on the floor.

"We need to get the door sealed up," Riley said. "And you need to get out of here if—"

"I thought I was leaving. But I'm not."

Riley understood, at least a little bit. Whatever it was—Dean Mitchell, whatever—it hadn't hurt her. Just the door. And if it somehow *had been* Dean, something was obviously wrong with him. And he was her husband.

"I'll help you with the door," Riley said, "then I'm going to look around. Get out of here if you feel unsafe. Call 911, call me, but get out."

Katelyn agreed.

The two women went upstairs and pulled a full sheet of plywood out of an unfinished portion of the attic. Katelyn found a cordless drill and some screws.

They screwed the door shut and placed the plywood over the inside to add another layer of defense.

The job took less than ten minutes, but Katelyn was visibly exhausted when they were done.

"I've been packing. I really thought I was leaving. I'm so tired."

Riley nodded. And again, she reminded her: "If it's an emergency, call 911. Then me. If you decide to leave, you can come to my place. Or go to a hotel in Harrison. Something."

A few minutes later, Riley drove slowly by Dean Mitchell's office, which appeared dark and locked up.

His truck was not in the alleyway, but she pulled in anyway and checked the back.

Nothing unusual that she could see.

She returned to her Jeep and began a slow and aimless course through Ellingwood, up and down the community's half-mile stretch of highway, then its side streets. The snow flurries from earlier in the evening had become a light sleet. Nobody was outdoors. Nobody was driving.

She was crawling to a near stop in front of Savannah Golding's house when a bright and swollen moon broke for less than a second through the clouds just a few inches above a grove of nearby trees. Now she *did* stop the Jeep. Put it in park.

Goddamn, what was she thinking? Nothing. Nothing at all.

But Dean Mitchell had perhaps seen his wife tonight… and he wasn't at his office, so could he be here? Yes.

Savannah's Camry was under the carport and a light was on at the end of the house.

Riley shut off the Jeep and got out.

There was a foul odor about the place, she thought immediately. Like body odor.

Riley went to the front door and rang the bell. Knocked, waited, and rang the bell again.

Nothing.

What in the *world* was that smell?

Riley knocked one more time and decided to look around.

The north end of the house appeared undisturbed. The dormant grass crunched with a thin layer of snow and sleet, no sign of footprints or any sort of recent activity. The back was much the same. All was still. But the south end of the house was a different story. A trail of faint tracks was mashed into the ice and brittle grass; the trail emerged from the edge of the property and became an unorganized mess right below the house's only glowing window—the glass of which was lined with cracks from a blow that had been delivered, judging by the pane's slight convex bulge, from the inside.

Riley stood back away from the window and the path of footprints.

Call. Right now. Sheriff Palmer.

Instead, she called Savannah's name, and when she got the response she knew she'd get, she returned to her Jeep and retrieved an old Starbucks gift card she kept in a lock pick set beneath the driver's seat. She used the card to open the back door. Stepped in. Drew her gun.

Silence.

She'd entered into the living room. The lights were off. The room was still.

She called Savannah's name. Nothing.

"Mr. Mitchell?"

Still nothing.

The lit up bedroom with the broken window was the master bedroom, down the hall from the makeshift office and storage room. The door was closed. Light leaked out onto the hallway floor beneath it.

Riley proceeded to the door and tapped her knuckles against it.

"Savannah?"

Again, no answer, and Riley opened the door.

Savannah was on the floor in front of the window with a baseball bat at her feet. She was in a night gown, face up, arms spread wide.

Riley crossed the floor in two steps, knelt next to her, nudged her shoulders, said her name, and finally felt for a pulse, which was not there.

The broken window—cracked and bulging outward—was the only sign of violence. There was nothing about this woman's body to indicate she'd been attacked or involved in a struggle.

Riley stood.

Sleet *tick tick ticked* against the window.

She stepped out in the hallway and retrieved her phone from her jacket.

10

ROBERT HAWKINS HAD GONE TO work for the Ozark-St. Francis National Forest almost twenty years ago, and he'd been behind the counter of the Harrelston station for the last eight. Standing or sitting behind this counter was a sort of semi-retirement, a way to keep himself active and engaged without the physical and mental stresses that came with being a full-time ranger. He was seventy-one. His joints had been bad since he was fifty. He still had good spells, and during those times, he could still hit the trails with the best of them. Sometimes he felt like he could coach high school basketball again! But those good spells lasted, what? Two weeks at most? Then it was back to the perpetual throbbing and burning, joints so sore and stiff he sometimes struggled with putting on his pants.

The Harrelston station kept him busy and in touch with the world. And Ellingwood had been his childhood home. He'd only moved away when he was in his twenties and thirties to get educated and teach and coach. Then there'd been his brief stint as a ranger out in Colorado. But home was home. It was familiar and peaceful. And the job wasn't difficult, either. He answered the phone, kept the place up, sold the occasional hat or tee shirt, and warned hikers who came in for advice to watch out for ticks and copperheads.

Now, sometimes there *was* excitement. Like the kid who'd smoked dope and walked right off a bluff into Oakwood Pond. Robert could look back on that episode with a smile, because he'd been feeling good then; he'd helped find the little fool, had wandered way out into cottonmouth territory to find him sprawled on the shore, okay except for a broken wrist.

Perhaps the *most* excitement his little corner of the Ozarks had seen was four years ago, when a convict had escaped from the prison in Newport, well over two hours away, but the convict was headed straight for the hills, trying to "get off the grid" (as he'd told his prison buddies), hoping to bushwhack his way to Missouri and then to God knows where. They found signs of him less than ten miles from the Harrelston station, but all Robert could do was cuss his arthritis and help the authorities understand the maps and the terrain. He was good with a map, had specifically mentioned a few nearby features that tended to draw people to them, especially bushwhackers looking for landmarks, and maybe that was how they found the nutjob out near Roundtop Mountain.

Yes, there had been some exciting times. Robert looked back on those experiences with a smile, because they'd brought a jolt to his standard routine… and in retrospect, both of them had been harmless enough.

Unlike now.

There was *nothing* to actually indicate Marion Golding was hurt, yet he couldn't help but think she was dead. Marion was a good kid, a hard worker; she loved her job, and most of the time, she loved her mother. She'd talked to Robert several times over the years about her life, and except for a few recent, innocent grumblings about her parents, Marion hadn't displayed the faintest interest in running off. She didn't even have a car!

Too much time had passed. No sign of the girl. She *had* to be dead, and the least Robert could do, he thought, was find her. He'd spent most of his waking hours (and a good portion of his sleep) combing over maps, trying to stumble upon something, anything, a new idea, a cavern, cabin, creek, river, or ravine that might have been neglected in all the searching.

Marion woke him up this morning (though he couldn't confidently say he'd ever fallen asleep to begin with). He sat up in bed (a lonely bed, as it had always been)… rubbed his eyes… and she was there, standing ghost-like by his television. Again, he rubbed his eyes, and she still didn't go away.

It's horrible, Robert.

What?

Being dead.

Why are you still here?

It's what killed me.

Tell me.

76

But she didn't, because that's when he realized she wasn't there.

So, he was making an earlier than usual drive to the station, long before the sun was up, because his mind was burning with thoughts of Marion Golding. *Dead.* There was an idea somewhere inside him. He needed to study his maps.

I'll find you, Marion. Promise.

Just know this isn't the kind of excitement I like.

A cold rain was falling—mixed with sleet, Robert was pretty sure—when he pulled into the station's gravel lot.

He pulled his Ranger into his normal space at the back of the lot, shut off the engine, zipped his jacket, pulled up the hood.

When he got out of the truck, a stench hit him.

He stuffed his hands in his pockets. Kicked the truck door shut. And approached the front of the station.

He could barely see the little building through the dark rain.

There it is. There's the stink. Oh my living God.

He stood in the lot and listened to the rain and sleet pelt against his hood.

She was sitting against the wall to the left of the door. Pale face toppled onto her left shoulder, legs crossed, hands in lap. She sat so casually, looking straight ahead, seeing nothing at all, because she was dead. Soaked. A corpse sprinkled with sleet.

He blinked, rubbed his eyes, checked again, and it was all the same. This was not a hallucination or a dream. She was there.

He dug out his keys and unlocked the door, rushed inside—or was he floating? All of this felt surreal, dreamlike. Light, he needed light, and he fumbled around on the wall to the right of the door till he found the switch. Flipped it, and thank God the nightmare wasn't in here, too.

IN THE MIDST OF THE ensuing chaos, after he'd spoken to Sheriff Palmer and provided a written description of exactly how he found Marion Golding's body, Constable Riley Saunders, who'd arrived less than a minute after the sheriff, pulled him aside and offered him a cup of coffee from the thermos in her Jeep. He accepted, and they sat in her Jeep for several quiet minutes, drinking coffee and watching the coroner, the sheriff, and a number of deputies scurry through the rain like lost rodents.

"Do you know what else happened last night?" Riley finally said.

"Here?"

"In town."

"No."

"Katelyn Mitchell's front door got hit so hard by someone or something that it broke the door frame. And Savannah Golding died last night. Looks like somebody or something came to her window and scared her to death—literally. They think she died of a heart attack."

"Marion's mother is dead?"

"Late last night. Whatever she saw, I'd say it was here, too."

11

DEAN MITCHELL PICKED HIMSELF UP off the ground. He was naked, cold, bruised, and bleeding. It was daylight now. The clouds were still spitting a steady mix of rain and sleet, and the limbs overhead did little to stop the precipitation from pelting him like dozens of stinging insects. He cursed and swatted and looked down at himself to confirm his nakedness. Probably he was on the brink of a breakdown, though he wasn't sure he could break any further.

Questions occurred to him once he was steady enough to face them: Where was he and why was he naked? There were no quick, obvious answers, and so, another question: What did he intend to do about it? He was in the woods now, obviously—somewhere in the woods. Going home, or to the office... impossible.

So keep going.

A flash of memory. Dean Mitchell, Attorney at Law, descending this hillside. Yes. And now, he tried to aim himself in the right direction, because the key was to *keep going*. He'd never get anywhere going in circles. Just like he'd never get anywhere in panic. Never get anywhere if he lost his cool. Move. Just move. Before the cold got the best of him.

He put his right foot forward.

Because he needed out of here, needed his clothes, needed his truck. Needed to remember and understand.

HE ALMOST REMEMBERED HITTING HER. It might've returned to him, this memory, when he reached back and touched the wound on his neck. It felt different; it wasn't so raw. It felt like it had become a permanent part of him.

He walked. He attempted to follow a path, if there was one. He attempted to ignore the cold, attempted to understand what was bubbling up in the back of his head.

What am I?

Something was very much *wrong*, but his thoughts weren't firing in any language he'd heard before, just blind, angry bursts of instinct. If he knew anything at all, it's that he'd seen the girl's face, and there was that fleeting burst of humanity that somehow came round again, and he'd grabbed her by her feet.

Before that?

Yesterday, before the nighttime insanity, he thought he'd tried to see a doctor. Because the day before...

80

He was *human* now, wasn't he? Yes, goddamn it, *yes*, so as he kept his feet moving (they weren't even cold now), he asked himself: *Where are my memories?* Answer: *They're returning slowly.* Yesterday, he hadn't *tried* to see a doctor... he *had* seen a doctor. The one right outside of Harrison. Because he was scared. Because the day before yesterday, he'd hit Katelyn. He recalled it. He assumed it was true. It wasn't all his fault. The thing on his neck. The things in his head. All that.

"Insane."

Right after he spoke it, he heard voices from behind him.

These thoughts could wait. Somebody was coming for him. He knew that. Because... he wasn't far from where he'd dragged the body. He'd passed out in a very bad spot, and now they were close.

He sprinted off the path, if there was a path, like he knew exactly where he was going, when all he really knew was that this was absurd and would most definitely *end* badly. He descended a steep slope that cut his feet (not that he felt it), nearly tripped on a rock, a root, something, regained his composure, kept going, and came to a narrow creek at the bottom. He turned left and rushed alongside the creek, quickly realized he was leaving footprints in the mud, and skirted up the slope to drier ground.

He kept going.

Eventually, he spotted a structure up ahead. As he drew closer to it, he heard a human voice coming from somewhere on the property.

He moved toward it, thinking *maybe* he could get his bearings.

No sprinting, though. Swiftly, silently. He did not know where he was or who owned this land. He did not know who all was behind him or how close they were.

Swiftly, silently, he more or less followed the creek toward what he eventually discerned was a mobile home. Every step closer revealed another unkempt detail. And something about the remains of a lightning-struck oak tree at the edge of the property brought about an information dump that was so potent it registered, briefly, as a blinding headache.

He remembered *almost everything* now, and the gaps in his memory that did exist were insignificant.

This property, he suddenly knew, belonged to an old fellow named Elmer Kopps. He remembered—clearly—seeing Kopps one day, years ago, at the Home Depot in Harrison; Kopps had been looking for a chainsaw, and he'd told everybody in the store about the lightning bolt that had nearly taken out his home.

Harmless old man, Dean Mitchell thought, as ignorant and uneducated as a lightning-blasted tree stump.

And there he was, stepping out his back door, dressed in boots and tattered old khakis and a stained white undershirt. His face, even from this distance of at least fifty yards, was visibly consumed by cancerous leather, and what hair he had left hadn't been cut in at least a year. Still, harmless old man. Nice enough when he bothered to show himself in civilization.

So why am I thinking what I'm thinking?

Naked desperation.

There were several means to achieve the goal he'd just set for himself, but all of them, save one, seemed far too risky.

So he simply acted.

He selected from the creek bed a pleasantly heavy, smooth, softball-sized rock. Bounced it in his right hand, clenched it tightly, and felt vine after vine of mental poison ivy creeping up his insides.

There was no fence around Kopps's property. Dean Mitchell remained low as he positioned himself behind the old fool, who was knelt down in his back yard, looking at a truck tire.

Dean Mitchell moved past a forgotten flowerbed, crossed the yard much more quietly than he thought possible, and brought the rock around just as Elmer Kopps was standing up. It was a sad, simple *thunk*, and that's all it took. The old man dropped to the weedy muck of his lawn, deader than any truck tire.

A sour gulp of acid arose from Dean Mitchell's stomach, but it was over and done with in one silent belch. He removed the old fool's clothes and put them on.

Even though he'd never felt less civilized, he was, at least for now, human again.

12

KATELYN MITCHELL AWOKE AT TEN 'o clock that morning, took one look at what used to be the front door, and knew that she was not going to Nashville. She'd known this all along, if she was totally honest with herself. But the plywood certainly killed any lingering romantic thoughts of driving east with the window down and country music on the radio while her husband sat drinking alone in his sad, roach-infested office oasis.

The plywood reminded her that something was happening.

If her apparently insane husband wanted to show back up and finish off what was left of their marriage, she intended to be here.

After last night, she *wanted* to see him. She wanted answers.

And she wanted to be prepared.

She showered and dressed and brewed half a pot of coffee and poured it into one of her husband's Yeti tumblers. She then checked her appearance in the half-bath mirror, because suddenly, she wasn't sure if she was fit to leave the house. She was cold and hot; she *had* to be feverish. Her eyes burned. And she was suddenly sure—though she'd *just* gotten done in the bathroom—that her face looked like hell again.

But according to the mirror, she looked... pretty much okay. Her eyes were clear and alert. Her color was healthy. She did not *look* ragged or feverish. The welt just below her right eye was the only conspicuous flaw on her face; it was purple and midnight blue and various shades of green, but it wasn't *big*.

And she was not going to damn herself to a cave until it went away.

SHE DROVE NORTH OUT OF Ellingwood to a sporting goods store in Harrison. She went to the back of the store to the guns and ammunition counter and told the sales associate she needed a home defense gun stronger than a .22 but light enough she could wield it comfortably. Ultimately, after debating between an intimidating 20-gauge and a Mossberg .410, she selected the latter. The sales associate told her the manager's wife had the same gun. Katelyn wasn't sure she believed this, but it didn't matter.

She purchased the Mossberg, a box of shells, and a deer camera. After placing her purchases in the back of the Honda, she crossed the parking lot to a Burger

King, where she ate a light lunch and attempted to sort her thoughts.

Would Dean return tonight? She had no idea. Had the thing in the lawn last night really been him? Yes, she thought. Somehow. And the door? It probably *hadn't* been knocked open with a single blow. She'd just *heard* one and missed the others because of shock or fear or adrenaline or something. Those marks on the door? They could be anything. Same thing, she suddenly thought, with the figure in the yard. It had been more or less shaped like a man. Anything suggesting it *wasn't* a man had to be credited to her imagination. And so it *was* a man, and with that settled, it was Dean—who else would it be?

She believed all this. Absolutely. But her newfound confidence in such sane explanations did not totally ease her mind. Her husband had hit her one night and knocked in the front door the next.

Of *course* she was frightened.

ON THE WAY BACK TO Ellingwood, Katelyn rounded a bend in the highway and somehow spotted a faint, quick glimmer of blue, first visible through the lower right corner of the windshield, then through the passenger window. Just as soon as it was there, it was gone.

Why she turned around, she didn't know, not at the time. But she checked her mirrors, slowed down, and executed a U-turn in the middle of the highway. She drove less than a quarter of a mile back to where she *thought* she'd seen the blue glimmer... and it was still

86

there, not even a hundred yards off the road, hidden—
for the most part—by a swell in the land.

She pulled onto the shoulder and parked.

Tire tracks, too, she thought, leaning into the
window. *Right across the field. You wouldn't notice them if you
weren't looking.*

She retrieved her phone from the passenger seat,
checked for traffic, and stepped out.

The highway wasn't even twenty feet behind her
when she realized that this mysterious glimmer was her
husband's truck. She'd probably known it long before
she doubled back and came all the way out here.

When she was close enough to be certain, she took
out her phone and called Riley Saunders.

The truck was empty.

And the driver's door was still standing open.

13

THERE WERE TIMES, MANY TIMES, when Constable Riley Saunders truly enjoyed her law enforcement position. She was under no illusions of self-importance; she sought no trouble or drama and usually received none. It was something to do, a way to serve her community, and even though she was a small woman with a modest, introverted personality, the position somehow suited her well, and she let herself believe that she was *good* for this job, good for this community, *because* she sought no glory.

And it was a good position. She was her own boss. She could spend time at the cafe, though she rarely needed to. The Painted Lady was the manager's baby and had been for years. Riley Saunders, more often than not, was just a name on a beneficiary deed. She spent most of her time doing *this*.

And what was *this*?

For now, it was a missing lawyer and his discarded Silverado.

She called Palmer and a wrecker and walked Katelyn back up to her car, explaining that she—Riley—was a few miles out of her jurisdiction and the sheriff would want a few lines from her.

Palmer arrived, looking as if he needed a drink and a week of sleep. Riley followed him down into the field and watched him take a stroll around the truck.

"You believe how that poor girl looked?" He took a sip of coffee from a foam Painted Lady cup.

Riley assumed he was talking about Marion Golding. Who else? Riley had left the ranger station over two hours ago, but Marion's body slumped so casually against the front of the building—so *dead*—was not an image that would be leaving her memory anytime in this lifetime.

"So now the lawyer's missing," Palmer said.

"Do you think there's a connection?"

"Between the lawyer and Marion?"

"Between Mitchell and anything."

"Dean Mitchell didn't kill Marion Golding. Daddy killed Marion Golding, then killed himself."

"I agree."

"Asshole lawyer's problems are his own. That's what I think." He leaned into the truck. "That prick'll be back. We're not lucky enough for him to not be."

"Last night?"

Palmer withdrew from the truck. "What about it?"

"Could he be connected to anything that happened last night?"

"Let's see." He leaned against the side of the Chevy. "Savannah Golding was a heart attack waiting to happen. But it looked like somebody was peeping in on her, scared her into it. A kid, I figure. The lawyer was getting it with her anyway, from what I've heard, so why would he need to peek?"

Riley admitted she had no idea.

Palmer continued: "I figure he knocked in his wife's door. Looks like he roughed her up recently, so that fits. My guess on what happened here? He was boozing up in Harrison and drove off the road. Left his truck cause he knew there's no way in hell it'd make it back up to the highway. Happened probably yesterday. That makes sense. You can see the tire tracks across there."

"And Marion Golding?"

"You're a smart lady. Give me any reason in the world why Dean Mitchell would drag Marion's body up to that ranger station."

"Why would anybody?"

"You got me there. You looked around yet?"

And the sheriff set off into the field.

PALMER, RILEY HAD TO ADMIT, was handy with logic. If a simple explanation exists, why not go with that one? Why make anything complicated when it doesn't have to be? Why make assumptions?

Riley considered his ideas as she followed Katelyn back to Ellingwood.

She agreed that Nathaniel Golding killed his daughter before killing himself. She couldn't help but

90

agree that Savannah Golding died of a heart attack; after all, *that's what happened.* She agreed that Dean Mitchell was the one who knocked down his wife's door, and she agreed that he'd probably been on his way back from Harrison yesterday when he went off the road.

She *disagreed* that it was a "kid" who scared Savannah to death. As a catch-all, she disagreed with Palmer's idea that Dean Mitchell's involvement in last night's events began and ended with his assault on his own front door. Palmer, she thought, would agree with her if he'd put down his philosopher's razor and consider the big picture.

And Palmer didn't know about the silver bullets. Why not? Why hadn't she told him?

All these recent events, Riley believed, were attached to the central core that was Nathaniel Golding's suicide. Or maybe that was wrong. Maybe the core was somehow the Evenware House? She did not let this thread distract her. Focus. There were connections between Dean Mitchell and Nathaniel Golding. Mitchell was representing Savannah Golding in their divorce, and he'd perhaps slept with her. He'd gone out to the Evenware House. He was the one who found Nathaniel's body.

So. If she believed Dean Mitchell was exclusively responsible for last night's trifecta of weirdness—and she did—what narrative could explain that?

The sore on his neck. Golding's silver bullets. The claw mark on the door.

There were pieces to this that Palmer either didn't have or wasn't considering.

Riley wasn't sure she wanted to think about them, either.

LESS THAN TEN MINUTES AFTER leaving Sheriff Palmer, Riley and Katelyn were sitting on Katelyn's front steps.

"Please don't repeat any of this. At some point or another, this *will* sound crazy." Riley paused, looking for the courage to dive in. "Two weeks before your husband found him dead, Nathaniel Golding went online and bought custom made silver bullets, .32 caliber, just what he needed for the gun he used to kill himself. There were three cartridges in the box I found. One was missing. We know a bullet went through his head, but we've yet to find it. I am *almost* certain the bullet he used to kill himself was the missing silver bullet. The shell casings match, but that doesn't tell everything. There are only a million bullets out there cased in nickel-plated brass."

Katelyn immediately jumped on the obvious question: "Why would he order silver bullets to kill himself?"

"Good question, isn't it?" Again, Riley paused. "Has Dean ever hit you before?"

Katelyn, after feigning interest in her fingernails, said no. "Our marriage hasn't been *healthy* in a long time. But he's never hit me. Till the night before last."

"I talked to Savannah Golding not long before she died. She said Nathaniel and Marion's relationship hadn't been great, but she gave no indication that he might've done anything to her."

"So…?"

92

"So. Nathaniel spends time at the Evenware House, *likely* kills his daughter, then kills himself. Your husband goes out to the Evenware House, then hits you for the first time in your marriage and disappears."

"So, something about the old house."

"Maybe. Also, consider this. This is where I remind you not to repeat what I'm saying." *Courage*, she thought. *Deep breath.* "Nathaniel bought those silver bullets, apparently so he could kill himself. Your husband found him on Monday, January 16. At the time he found him, Nathaniel had been dead for no more than four days."

"Okay?"

"He killed himself—and Marion, I'd wager right now—on or around January 12. The full moon."

Katelyn turned to face her. Her mouth cracked open. Her eyes froze and widened.

Riley said: "I looked at a lunar calendar on my phone. Last night, when all the craziness happened, was *basically* a full moon, over ninety-nine percent illumination. Tonight *is* the full moon."

"Constable. You're not seriously saying what this sounds like." She faked a laugh. "That's ridiculous."

"Call me Riley, please. Given the nature of this conversation, I think we're on a first name basis. I'm not suggesting that something any sane person would regard as impossible is true. I guess I'm suggesting that *insane* people might believe it."

"I've never thought of Dean as insane. Cruel, maybe. But not insane."

"Savannah Golding might've said the same thing about Nathaniel."

93

"But Dean was never that way! Does that just happen? Are you normal one day and shooting yourself with silver the next?"

"I don't know. Forget how impossible it sounds to *us*. Think about it in summary: It's a safe bet Nathaniel killed Marion, and it's a safe bet he killed her shortly before he killed himself. It's also a safe bet that he shot himself with the missing silver bullet. This was all on or extremely close to a full moon. Next full moon? Insanity again, partially or one-hundred percent performed by your husband. Both men were out at the Evenware House, which Nathaniel was tearing down—because Mary thought it 'unsafe,' we've been told. Ignore what you and I believe can or can't be true. We aren't the ones doing any of this. Maybe there isn't a trend yet, but tonight could tell the tale, and you need to be careful—tonight. Surely you agree with that."

"Of course I do. Are you thinking they got something out there, like *sick*? That thing on his neck? That makes some sense. But why the full moon and silver bullet business? That's silly. It's absurd."

"To *us*. Right now, I'm just anxious about tonight."

14

WHEN HER CRIES BEGAN, LEWIS Evenware was engulfed in the kind of bland, uneventful afternoon that had become a staple of his existence: he was upstairs in his room, browsing the internet, wondering, in the back of his mind, why the Good Lord had made him so bland, why it was *his* responsibility to take care of his mother. He was forty. He had things to do! Except for when he didn't, which was frequently. His life was nothing but his mother and his distractions: the internet, the video games, the books and puzzles. He was not miserable. He did not pity himself. He just wondered... Why had he moved back home all those years ago, letting all those college credits go to waste? Too lazy to finish? Too low on ambition? Too scared of work and taxes? Lately, though, since the big decision to tear down the old house, he'd begun to understand: it was his mother. He worried for her. She was rooted here, would leave only in death. *And there were wicked things here.* Maybe he'd blocked them from his brain, for the sake of sanity. But that did not in any way undo their existence.

Such were his thoughts when her cries began. Her voice crept out of the first floor den, floated up the stairs, and made it to his ears with barely an ounce of power left in it.

She was calling his name. This was not normal. She seldom said anything at all. Since her marbles started leaking, she typically sat in an eerie, ethereal silence, no matter how content or miserable her state. She'd *never* called to him. Never. He initially thought he might be mistaken.

But no.

"Lewis."

No question mark or exclamation point at the end. She spoke simply of an insignificant object.

He closed the laptop and paced over to his bedroom door. Maybe she was just having a spell and would quit; maybe she didn't actually need anything.

If she did, he wasn't sure he wanted to hear it.

"Lewis."

He cursed, maybe aloud, and descended to the den. She was as she should be: in her chair, which was positioned near the window so she could look out at their vast lawn. Which is exactly what she was doing. She wasn't looking for him or at him. She did not seem to need anything. He felt a twinge of irritation, but suppressed it, reminding himself that this kind old lady who'd lost track of reality was his *mother*. That he was here watching her blink out of existence was not in any way her fault.

Not looking away from the window, Mary Evenware said, "Lewis."

"Yes, Mom?"

He started across the floor.

Surprisingly, there *was* an answer. And for the first time in weeks, his mother sounded both aware and confident: "I need a paper and pencil, Lewis. Paper and pencil."

Lewis set off and gathered up a notebook and a pencil. When he returned, she reached eagerly for the items. She set them in her lap and was still. Lewis stood over her, wondering—for a second—if she'd died. Then her right hand established a grip on the pencil, and she put it to the paper.

"Lewis," she said, "would you leave me alone for a moment?"

He left the den and went into the kitchen, where he sat down at the dining table and drummed his fingers on the oak and accepted that this could not be good. He wanted to believe this was just another display of her failing mind, but he'd be lying to himself if he tried to believe this. For right now, she was not out of it. Her eyes were clear. She knew exactly who she was, who he was.

How long should I give her? Go back in there now? No, not yet. Wait till she calls me again?

But he feared she *wouldn't* call him back.

Still, he couldn't go back in there now. So he sat, drumming his fingers, waiting.

After several minutes, he stood, paced around the table, checked a few things on his phone that he didn't need to check, and sat down again. And damn it, at some point, enough was enough.

He reentered the den but hung back by the doorway. She was still there in the gray window light, tapping the pencil's eraser against the notebook in her lap. He watched, waited for her to stop tapping, to turn around and acknowledge him, to say something. But her mind had apparently returned to the ether. Tap, tap, tap. That's all she could do.

He crossed the floor and hung back a few feet from her wheelchair when the pencil stopped tapping.

"Mom?"

She did not turn to him. Nor did she respond in any meaningful way.

The pencil fell, landed softly on the carpet, and a strange noise that might have been a one-syllable version of his name crawled weakly out of her throat.

"Mom?" He stepped around to the front of her chair. "Are you okay?"

Her mouth was open and leaking something similar to his name again. The noise was accompanied by drool, and a similar fluid leaked from both of her nostrils. Her eyes were rolling erratically, like those of a broken doll. One hand began to thrash against the side of the chair, determined to find the pencil that was no longer there. She tried to speak again, attempted to lean forward, tried to rise, all the while making that noise. The whole time, that noise.

Then it all stopped.

A numb silence fell over the room.

He placed a hand over her mouth and nose and felt no breath. He felt for a pulse and found none. And shortly after he confirmed his mother was no longer alive, he saw that she'd actually written something in the notebook. Small print, right in the middle of the page.

He picked up the book and studied her work.

It was weak, arthritic, but also clear:

thomas wolf.

"What?" Lewis said.

Thomas Wolf? Had she died with a burst of literary inspiration and misspelled a favorite author's name? Lewis tried to recall if he'd ever seen her reading a book. Maybe? He wasn't sure. Certainly, he could not recall her reading a *Thomas Wolfe* novel. And he was positive there wasn't a book by that man anywhere in this house.

The writing was likely one last product of her mental haze, something perhaps not at all related to that certain twentieth-century novelist.

But did it mean something?

What he needed to do was go back upstairs and take a nip of the whiskey he kept at his bedside. Then, he needed to cry. Just a little bit. Because this was his mother, and the years and images and scoldings and smiles were returning to him, and she was done. After that, it was time to call it in.

Time to tell the world his mother was gone.

15

L𝐀𝐓𝐄 𝐓𝐇𝐀𝐓 𝐀𝐅𝐓𝐄𝐑𝐍𝐎𝐎𝐍, P𝐀𝐋𝐌𝐄𝐑 𝐀𝐍𝐃 two of his deputies found Elmer Kopps in his back yard, wearing only his underwear. Dead from a blow to the head. Judging from the soggy blood and the urine in his briefs, he hadn't been dead all that long.

Robert Hawkins had spent the morning talking to Sheriff Palmer, and it had been Robert's idea for them to go down to the creek and follow it for a few miles.

As a result, they found Elmer sooner rather than later. They also found, on the slope between the creek and the station, a pink wool glove that matched one stuffed into Marion Golding's jacket. The discussion turned immediately as to whether or not Elmer's murder was connected to the death of Marion Golding and her body turning up at the ranger station.

"I don't even know how a *human* could've done that," Robert heard one of the deputies say that afternoon. "Did you see how her stomach was torn open?"

Robert had thought something similar when he first saw the girl's body. But coming from the deputy, the sentiment resonated even more potently.

The paradox, Robert thought, was that, *yes*, there had to be a link between Marion's death and that of Elmer Kopps, but *no*, there was nothing similar about their deaths and no apparent connection between the two people at all, other than Elmer's relatively close proximity to where Marion's corpse had washed ashore.

Late that afternoon, after everyone was gone, Robert left the station and went down to the End Zone to have a Miller and sort his thoughts. He sat alone at the end of the bar and watched the bartender mix drinks and run drafts, and he thought about the piece of shit who'd killed Elmer Kopps. Elmer hadn't been anything at all. Why kill him? What did it mean? The beer didn't have any answers, but Lord, it helped him think. Elmer Kopps. Marion Golding. Right there where he worked. He decided he'd go down to the creek. They were missing something. *He* was missing something.

You're a hell of a resource, Robert, Palmer had told him a few hours ago. *Is there anything about this area you don't know?*

Yes. *This.* Whatever it was. He'd go down to the creek, and probably nothing would happen, and he wouldn't think of anything. But maybe!

He drank a second beer, paid his tab, and drove back to his house. The sky was dim with faint orange dusk light as he stuffed his coffee thermos, .30-06, and a box of ammunition into his Ranger and started back toward the station. By the time he pulled off the highway onto a dirt road about two hundred yards from the station's driveway, the pale silver glow of the February wolf moon was expanding through the narrow woods that separated this road from the station's parking lot.

He'd come here, to this road, because he didn't want to announce his presence at the station. He parked on the side of the road, got out, and urinated into the darkness. Then—jacket zipped, ammunition and flashlight tucked in its pockets, rifle over his back—he started into the trees. He'd check out the station first, then go down to the creek.

The woods were not very thick, and the rising moon lit his way.

When the station came into view, he slowed and ultimately stopped about twenty feet from the line where the trees gave way to the gravel parking lot. The little brown building was there, a shadow with no details. He knelt down to rest. And watch.

This was Robert's workplace, and he'd worked with Marion for almost two years. He felt a duty to *not* sit on his ass. Sure, Palmer was a nice guy. But he was the sheriff of one of the least populated counties in a very rural state. He knew what he was doing, sometimes. He was driven and determined and ambitious, when he wanted to be. Usually, though, when a significant crime befell this corner of the hills (which *did* happen with sparse regularity), there was no resolution until the resolution grew impatient and reminded Palmer of its existence (and location) with a sharp whack to the sheriff's head.

One of Palmer's deputies would patrol this area tonight. A time or two. Maybe good old Constable Riley Saunders would pull in and sit a while. But what were the odds that the shit show, should it come, would play itself out in the cones of their headlights?

The moon was over the treetops now.

The yellow tape near the station's front door fluttered in the night's chilling breeze.

The whole scene was empty and silent.

Several minutes passed, then half an hour, then more. The moon rose higher, the cold sank deeper, and Robert decided he'd kept watch long enough. For now at least. He still wanted to go down to the creek, anyway, because *that's* what had been driving him crazy.

He returned to his truck, lowered the tailgate, and sat for a moment.

He felt anxious. It was natural, maybe, given the circumstances. But his heart was thumping, and he was sweating in the cold, and he did not want to admit that it was because of the moonlight.

Bullshit, he thought.

One last drink of coffee, and he put the lid back on the thermos, urinated again, and set off down the road. North, toward the creek. This road actually wasn't much of a road at all, but it provided a logical, easy-to-follow path—albeit one much too rock-studded and rutted for his little Ranger.

The road ended abruptly where the land dropped off at roughly forty-five degrees toward the creek.

The water was visible, glistening in the darkness like a vein of diamonds.

This was one of the steepest points on the slope; he could cut probably a hundred feet to his left or right and find terrain much less likely to twist his ankles.

He was pondering this—just going to the left, toward a thicket of brush and cedar trees—when he heard it, to his right, in the woods… twigs snapping, leaves crunching, followed by silence, but not for long.

The noises came again.

Robert retreated a few steps and slung the rifle around and muttered a curse that he could see absolutely *nothing* in the trees; where there should have been moonlight there was only a wall of blackness. Or maybe that was panic clouding his vision? Panic, yes, because *something* was in those woods, and it sounded *big*, and he'd consider running, if he thought it wouldn't be a death sentence.

As it was, the .30-06 was the safer bet.

Probably just an animal anyway. What are you afraid of?

The *snapping* and *crunching* grew steadier and louder, and the noises were soon accompanied by raspy breathing.

Robert forced himself to stand his ground. He raised and readied the rifle and peered into the darkness straight ahead.

There it is.

A featureless black smudge at first, more or less human in shape, yet obviously *not* human. Then, a face emerged, as if rising from dark water; the snarl, the eyes, the teeth, the snout—an animal, lanky yet obviously powerful, rushing in on two legs.

Robert fired.

The round hit home and the incoming threat collapsed in an explosion of splatter. Moonlight returned and revealed a sizable portion of its face painted on a nearby tree.

Though his heart was racing, Robert felt amazingly calm as he lowered the rifle and blinked away a droplet of warm splatter that wanted in his eye. He prepared to step toward whatever the hell it was he'd just shot down. But his calmness fled immediately when the thing leapt up, howled in pain—yes, *howled*—and fled toward the creek, somewhere down deep into the darkness. It stumbled at first, using its arms as well as its legs for the first few yards of its escape, but it was nevertheless vanished before Robert totally registered what had just happened.

I just shot the thing in the face. He had blood on him! He'd seen (in slow motion, he swore to God) a portion of its head disappear.

So he stood silently, his mouth partially open, wondering if his ears were really ringing, if the splatter he'd felt was real, if *anything* was real. Had he shot the gun? Had he shot at nothing?

He knelt down. Breathed deeply. Listened. Touched a fingertip to his face, confirmed the cool dampness of the blood.

It *had* been there. He knew it. And it was long gone.

Breathe, he thought. *That's all you've got to do. Breathe.*

16

KATELYN AND RILEY ATTACHED KATELYN'S new deer camera to a pine at the front edge of the property, so that it would capture the front of the house and most of the front lawn. This done, Riley examined and congratulated Katelyn on her new Mossberg. They took the gun into the back yard and test fired it.

Katelyn supposed she should have been pleased with all of this, but why? In what reality was the thought of shooting a sick and insane version of her husband appealing? *Should it be necessary. Surely it wouldn't be necessary.*

Shortly after their work with the camera and gun, while they were in the living room conversing, there was a knock on the back door.

It was Sheriff Palmer. He stood on the back step, in uniform, hat on his head, thumbs in his belt loops.

"Hello, Katelyn. Constable."

"Sheriff," Katelyn said.

"If you don't mind." He nodded at Katelyn. She apologized and stepped out of his way. He entered the house, removed his hat, and crossed over to the couch, where he sat down across from Riley.

He took a quick glance at the boarded up front door, then said: "So I've made some discoveries and have been thinking."

Katelyn sat back down next to Riley.

"First of all," Palmer said, glancing at Riley, "a confession. I wasn't sure you'd be here, Constable, but I'm glad you are. I must confess, I've accepted that, last night, a bunch of stuff happened, and your husband is missing, Katelyn, and I can't think of anybody else to blame anything on. I still have no idea what in the world Dean Mitchell has to do with Marion Golding's body, unless he killed her. And maybe he did. I still don't know why he would've been outside Savannah's window, but maybe he was. We just found his clothes, way out in the woods, close to his truck. I have a picture on my phone…."

He extended his phone to Katelyn and asked her to confirm that the torn and dirty articles looked like Dean's.

She nodded.

"Second of all," Palmer continued, "it's not just Marion anymore. We found Elmer Kopps, dead. In his yard. Killed with a rock to the head."

"Elmer Kopps?" Katelyn said.

Riley sat deathly still, showing no emotion at all.

"Now, am I missing something?" Sheriff Palmer leaned forward, wadded his hands together. "I need you two to talk to me. Katelyn, your husband *is* connected to this dead family, isn't he? He was working on Nathaniel and Savannah's divorce."

"Yes."

"What about Elmer Kopps? Any connection?"

Katelyn shook her head.

"Just proximity, then, to where Marion got left. *Maybe* close to where she died. So back to the present. I need *something* from one of you. I've got here in front of me the wife of a missing fella who's probably at the center of all it, and I've got our well-respected constable who no doubt is a hell of a lot smarter than I am. So tell me what I'm missing. I need motive, I need a narrative, I need a thread, somewhere to go, besides the goddamned woods—my immediate apologies."

Katelyn looked at Riley.

And Riley showed signs of life again. "Have you found any trace of the bullet Nathaniel shot himself with?"

"No. Strange, isn't it? But if you're thinking he didn't kill himself, it's obvious. He'd been holding the gun, as well as—"

"I know he killed himself. I was asking about the bullet."

The sheriff leaned in even closer.

"You've got something on your mind, Riley. I'm no psychiatrist or philosopher, but it's obvious. Let's help each other out."

A sincere plea, Katelyn thought, from a mostly good (if unremarkable) man who likely felt a bit in over his head.

"Any thoughts I have right now are pretty crazy," Riley said.

"Did you see Marion's body? Of course it's crazy. And now we have Elmer Kopps."

"I might know something about Nathaniel Golding, Sheriff." Riley was apparently going for it. Why not? "I think he was very, very disturbed. I think he shot himself with a silver bullet."

"Like a—?"

"Like in werewolf stories, yes. I talked to Savannah before she died. I was trying to find Marion, and I was looking for somewhere to begin. I had this not-so-crazy idea that it wasn't a coincidence that she went missing about the time her dad shot himself. Savannah more or less suggested he might've been looking at strange things on the computer. I found where he'd been to a custom weaponry website. And there was a box from that company in the top of his closet. .32 caliber silver bullets, just the ones he'd need for his pistol. It was supposed to contain three cartridges, but it only contained two."

Palmer acted like he was considering this. After a minute, he simply smiled and shook his head.

"But what does that explain? That Golding was insane? We've known that."

"What if he got *sick* out there, Sheriff, from something at the Evenware House? Which led him to kill his daughter, which led him to kill himself. Then, Dean goes out there, and here we go again. Somebody else is dead, and Dean is nowhere to be found."

Again, Palmer went quiet.

Until he stood, put on his hat, and said: "Thank you, ladies. I don't know what the hell is going on, but I need to do some more thinking."

109

17

WILSON PALMER HAD FIRST RUN for sheriff ten years ago, because he was drawn to law enforcement, and because he preferred a job and life that followed certain rules and procedures. He made a good sheriff, he figured. He was a pretty decent guy who didn't take any shit, but his refusal to take shit was born out of respect, not out of arrogance or feigned toughness. He was grounded. Rational. A personality thing, his daddy had told him. *You're not one for bullshit, boy. You live in the real world.*

And *movie monsters* weren't part of the real world. Palmer could not fathom the concept, nor anybody insane enough to indulge it. He'd spent a lifetime in this county, forty-seven years and counting, and he'd never, until now, encountered even the faintest *trace* of an absurdity like this one. Furthermore, he'd known Nathaniel Golding for nearly two decades. The man had always been a special sort of worthless, but never in all those twenty years had Palmer heard him talking about *monsters*.

Riley, God bless her, was a smart woman. He figured she probably led him by double digits in the IQ race, but he didn't give a single sort of damn about that, and it was looking now like she'd read a few too many books. Palmer had read a few good books in his life; he hadn't any problem with enjoying a crazy story every now and then, but he also believed that if you put a bunch of drivel *in*, you were bound to get some drivel *out*.

Such was the case, he thought, with Riley, who'd followed him out the door and now stood in front of him in Katelyn Mitchell's back yard. Crazy folks were out there; he could accept that. Monsters, he could *not* accept that. And the idea of a house *turning* people crazy was about as bad. The poor constable apparently read his thoughts right off his face; she looked like she was about to cry.

"I said *sick*, Sheriff Palmer. You can see for yourself."

Palmer didn't want to make anything worse, so he did the only thing he could do. He said a polite, quick goodbye, waved, and walked around to his car.

But when he got into his marked Explorer, he thought: *Just accept it. You're going to do exactly what she told you to do.*

And that's what he did.

WITH THE WHOLE FAMILY DEAD, it looked like the Golding property was going to go, according to

Savannah's will, to Savannah's older sister, who lived (last Palmer heard) in Springdale or Rogers or somewhere up there in the Walmart metropolis. Which meant there was likely nothing going on at the Golding's place, and it might be a good idea for the good sheriff to make sure the place was locked up.

And it *was* locked up. But maybe he should make sure nobody was pilfering through the dead folks' belongings before the judgment of Great God Probate.

He let himself in with a copy of the key he'd had since Nathaniel's final departure, and for a moment he actually pretended to care about the foyer, the den, the dining room; then he went back to the master bedroom.

Riley's read too many books. Even if Nathaniel did go a little bit weird and buy a box of silver bullets, what does that tell you, really? Nothing!

Oh yes? Well, here they were. Right at the top of the closet. Like Riley said.

You understand, don't you, Sheriff?

Somewhere deep within himself, Palmer admitted that the whole damned idea seemed a lot more plausible when you actually had a box of silver bullets in your hands.

You weren't really a wolf, Nathaniel. What in the blazing hell happened to you?

He removed a cartridge from the box, weighed it in his hand, held it up in front of his face, considered it... and tried to understand what madness might possess a man to waste money on such a thing. Horror nerds, maybe. But horror nerds wouldn't stash the things in their closets.

It *did* look like Nathaniel took himself out with one of these things. Had the crazy bastard thought himself the wolf man and gone Lone Ranger on his own brain?

Assume Riley is at least a little bit right. Nathaniel Golding started it and Dean Mitchell is somehow continuing it.

He put the bullet back in the box, put the box back on the shelf, and got the hell out of the house.

THE REMAINS OF THE EVENWARE House were malicious.

Palmer cursed himself for the thought. He'd never been this way, and he did not know why he was now. Malicious. As if a *house*, in any state, could reason, plan, act.

You don't know this house.

No, he didn't. He hadn't been the sheriff when old John Evenware supposedly disappeared and his wife and son abandoned the place. There'd been some rumblings about it throughout the community, but that had been in the nineties, when he was a much younger man, well before his official duties.

He hadn't given a damn then, and he wished he still didn't.

He parked alongside the last remains of the private drive, repeatedly reminding himself that the only thing he might see out here was an animal or a crazy lawyer who may or may not be a murderer. And Palmer was armed and ready. Right? Such were his thoughts.

They were almost convincing.

But when he was halfway up the yard, he saw movement in the house—*human* movement, he thought,

113

because the dark shape that had moved past the large, shattered window to the left of the front door had been a man. Or—

No, a man. He was sure of it.

He drew his gun, stood still, waited for it to happen again.

It did not.

Palmer cursed and finished the trek to the front door, pushed it inward, stepped inside. He called for Dean.

"This is Sheriff Wilson Palmer," he said. "If you're in here, I just want to talk to you."

But the house was empty. Just dust, trash… and a fairly random plant that was growing up between the floorboards in a far corner. Green still. A few light purple flowers. *In the wintertime?* Palmer thought.

He took a few steps towards the plant, and a smoky, male voice from the stairs to the right of the door said: "You won't find Dean Mitchell here. He's a fool, but he's not stupid."

Palmer spun around, and the shape of a man that was both there and not there stood in plain sight at the bottom of the stairs. *There and not there.* The shadows of the fading afternoon were as much a part of this specter as its flesh and clothes, and Palmer wasn't convinced that any of it was real. The figure looked old, but not ancient: stout frame, weathered face, unkempt gray hair.

"Who are you?" Palmer said.

"Nothing at all."

And with that, the shadows at the bottom of the stairs contained only a dust cloud that danced eerily in the gray light coming through the door.

18

RILEY INSISTED ON STAYING WITH Katelyn that evening, and they found themselves sitting outside her back door in two metal patio chairs as the moon rose. They were drinking coffee from insulated cups; both had their jackets zipped up to their chins. But neither minded the cold. They wanted to see the moon.

It *was* a beautiful sight, Riley thought. At its current location, hovering directly over the neighbor's roof, the details of its craters, canyons, and mountains seemed impossibly clear.

They hadn't spoken much since they'd come out here. They'd talked about life, the weather, The Painted Lady, Sheriff Palmer, what it was like being constable, cities, big towns, small towns… All while the moon was rising up from behind the neighbor's house. But now that it had gained a secure spot in the sky, they weren't so eager to speak.

Until Katelyn said: "I remember how he looked last night. I keep hoping I'll convince myself it was a dream, or bad lighting. But I saw enough. I remember."

Riley preferred not to think about this right now. It went with the moon much too well.

They were sitting in the silent aftermath of Katelyn's remembrance when a not-so-distant *crack* of a rifle sounded to the north. It didn't take much imagination to identify its general location.

"That didn't sound good," Riley said.

IT WAS LESS THAN TWO miles up the highway from Katelyn's street to the bend in the highway containing the ranger station.

Ellingwood was quiet this evening. Nobody else seemed to have taken note of the rifle blast. But this was rural Arkansas; of *course* nobody panicked at the sound of a rifle.

And it could be totally innocent, Riley thought. *There is still hope for that.*

Just before reaching the station, Riley spotted headlights down an old road that she was sure led to absolutely nothing.

She made the turn.

The source of the headlights proved to be Robert Hawkins's Ford Ranger. The old man was leaning against the side of the bed, staring into space... until he recognized Riley's Jeep. Then, he pulled himself away from the truck and approached the Wrangler as Katelyn rolled down the passenger window.

Riley noted that the Ranger's tailgate was down, and a large hunting rifle was laid across it.

"Did you just shoot?" Riley said.

Robert pointed further down the road. "Go on and look. The Jeep will make it."

Riley eased her foot off the brake and continued down the road, keeping it at a crawl.

Less than five minutes later, she put the vehicle in park, pulled a flashlight out of the glove box, and got out. Katelyn followed.

Riley had stopped for two reasons. One, because the vast darkness up ahead signaled the end of the road. Two, because what they were supposed to find was splattered all over the dirt and rocks in the middle of the Jeep's headlight beams.

Something dark. Blood? Yes, a galaxy of splatter.

But, Riley soon noted when she turned on her flashlight and aimed it into the woods, it wasn't *just* this substance.

She stepped into the trees and touched her fingers to one of the trunks.

What were these markings?

They were similar to those slashed across Katelyn's front door.

No. That was wrong. They were the same damned thing.

RILEY DROVE THEM OUT TO the End Zone.

Robert took off his blood-splattered jacket before going inside.

On this particular night, a Thursday, the one-room bar was less than half full, and they had no trouble finding a quiet table.

Riley went to the bar and got drinks—gin and tonics all the way around—and when she returned, Robert was rubbing his temples and Katelyn was smoking a cigarette she'd bummed off a young man at a nearby pool table.

Robert seemed to feel better after he took a few pulls from his drink. He took a deep breath and said: "I kept thinking I was missing something. I parked away from the station, there on that road, and I walked around. Went near the station for a while. Then went down the road. Had my gun, obviously. I wasn't too scared. I was going down to the creek. I thought something might happen. It came right at me."

"It?" Riley said.

Robert took the straw out of his cup and downed over half the gin and tonic in one gulp. "What could I call it that would make people believe me? I don't have any idea what it was. It was an animal, but it came at me like a man, on two feet, and say what you want, but it was human behind its eyes." He crunched an ice cube between his teeth. "And that isn't the bad part."

Katelyn stared into whatever void was at the end of her cigarette.

"I shot it," Robert said. "I didn't get it between the eyes, but I got its face. It *splattered* on me. You saw the blood. And it went down! Then it got back up and ran off like a kicked dog. That's impossible, but kill me now if I didn't watch it with my own eyes."

"Are you sure?" Riley said. "I don't mean that in *any* hurtful way, Robert. You know I trust you. But you got a good look at it? You're *sure?*"

"I'm not offended. You gotta know how many times I've asked myself that. The moon was a big old spotlight. I know what I saw."

They sat in silence.

Assume he's right, Riley thought. *Give it to him for now. What do you do? What's the next step?*

Return to the woods, she thought. Take a closer look. Get pictures.

Katelyn said: "That sounds like what I saw."

"You've seen it too?" Robert said.

"In my yard." As best she could, Katelyn described her front door crashing open, revealing the figure in her yard that hadn't *quite* been human. "I've spent the last twenty-four hours convincing myself it was just... Dean, with my imagination doing the rest. I'm not convinced now."

19

"IT BURNS," ROBERT SAID AS he pulled his truck into Katelyn's driveway.

Riley had requested they stay together. The thought of going somewhere else for the night, perhaps to a hotel in Harrison, had crossed their minds, but Katelyn refused. Whatever it was, Dean or not, she intended to be around. Riley hadn't put up much of a fight. *Just stay together*, she'd said. *I'll be there soon.*

"What burns?" Katelyn said.

"The blood. I didn't know I had this much on me, but I can feel every drop. It burns." He pulled the truck up as far as he could and shut it off. "I've got to get this off of me."

Once inside, Katelyn showed him to the bathroom and found him a tee shirt and a pair of sweatpants.

Next, she was standing over the couch in the den, looking down at the two objects lying there: their guns. They were comforting, in a surface-level sort of way.

From the neighbor's back yard, Doris began to bark. It was one of those mundane noises that barely sparked the brain.

Robert emerged from the bathroom. He looked better, almost well. And he didn't notice the barking, either, until it became evident that the creature wasn't going to quit.

Robert grabbed his rifle off the couch and crept toward the front window.

Katelyn stepped up beside him as he eased the curtain back.

The moon lit the night well, but not well enough to conquer the shadows cast by the pines at the edge of the yard. *Anything* could be in that darkness—including nothing.

But there was a slight shift in the shadows, and less than a second later, headlights—Riley's headlights, as it turned out—washed over the entire scene, revealing the shift for what it was. It was hunkered amongst the trees, squatting as if relieving itself, and it was trying to stand. One hairy hand grasped at a tree. Its bleeding, blasted head hung low. Foul fluid streamed from its mouth, first in a rush, then in a fine tendril. Its breaths were visibly heavy; each one sent its back arching into the air. How long this went on, Katelyn couldn't say. It could've been a minute, or it could've been five, but at some point, the vomiting stopped.

It threw its head back and emitted a pained, gurgling noise that was almost a howl, then lowered its

121

gaze and stared—for less than a second—straight into Riley's headlights. It succeeded in picking itself up, and with one gigantic claw, took a swipe at the air in front of it before bounding off into the darkness behind it.

Riley sprung out of her Jeep, leaving the door open and the headlights on, as Katelyn and Robert rushed out the back door and around the side of the house.

They'd all seen it.

In this way, they were all now connected.

They stood out in the cold moonlight, quiet, unmoving.

It took several minutes for the spell to break.

"I HAVE TO CALL PALMER," Riley said. "We have to warn people."

"And tell the truth?" Robert aimed a trembling finger at Katelyn's laptop, which was open before them on the dining table. On the screen was the best of the deer camera's images; it showed, clearly, a lanky, animal-like creature that was more or less covered in fur; it was a profile view, and the ghastly, seeping wound in the side of its head was right there in all its gory detail.

"He won't get the whole truth tonight," Riley said. "Tomorrow, maybe. Tonight, I can't."

20

S<small>HE TRIED TO TELL HIM.</small>

Riley met Palmer for breakfast at The Painted Lady early the next morning. The sheriff was quiet through the meal's first few minutes. He seemed to have an idea that he was in for one hell of a story.

"So what do I not know?" he said. "Last night, I heard all about somebody or something being back in Katelyn's yard. I heard Robert got attacked while he was nosing around out at the station. What else? It must be good, since it had to wait for daylight."

Palmer spoke most of this around a half-swallowed bite of toast, as if to emphasize how seriously he was taking things.

Riley was annoyed, but his attitude did not weigh heavily on her. She explained what she knew, mentioning the events lining up with the full moon, only because it's what she *had* to do. When she was done, she thought: *And if this were a perfect world, he'd find a way to*

123

believe me, and we'd all work together to solve the problem. But nothing was perfect and to hell with him if he wanted to be rude or dismissive.

"We all saw it," Riley concluded. "It wasn't a *man*, Sheriff. We couldn't say much last night. We were all stunned."

"You're *truly* saying this wasn't a human, this thing that attacked Robert and showed up in Katelyn's yard? I'm sorry, Riley."

Riley put down her fork and wiped her hands on her jeans. "You don't think Robert and Katelyn made this up. Or *me*. Do you?"

Palmer shrugged as he chewed. Then said: "Maybe a little? Probably not on purpose. I don't think Robert had any business up there. It was dark. I think *something* happened, or maybe he *thought* something happened. But I don't think he shot *something* in the face and then it got up and ran off. I can't accept that."

"He saw what he saw." She dug her fingernails into her legs. "He just didn't know how to tell you about it."

"Let's just get to the obvious, Riley." He took a sip of coffee. "There is no way in hell this is true. I like you. I trust you. I think you believe this, somehow. But Jesus Christ."

"Something got shot out there. Surely you saw the blood."

"I saw something. Sure as hell wasn't *human* blood. Looked more like gritty old oil."

"Sheriff. Please."

"I was prepared to believe you, about any number of things. You know what? I went out to the Evenware House yesterday and spooked myself quite a bit. I'm

124

kind of open minded. But tell me truly, Riley. God bless you. Are you *seriously* saying you folks saw a…" He looked around the diner. "A *werewolf?* Riley Saunders, come on now."

"I didn't say that. I'm not going to tell you what I think it is, because I don't know. But there's this."

She'd emailed the deer camera picture to herself last night. She pulled up the email and handed her phone to Palmer.

He looked at it for a moment and handed it back. "I have to trust logic more than a picture on a cell phone. I'm sorry."

"How can I blame you? It's crazy."

She meant it. She was still angry at his condescending tone. But she meant it.

Palmer sipped his coffee and stared at her over the cup. He set it down and shoved his plate away and said: "Do I suspect Dean Mitchell killed Elmer Kopps? Put Marion Golding out in front of the station? Among other things? Well, yeah, that's reasonable. Do I think the Evenware House is somehow in the middle of all this? Sort of. Could be Dean and Nathaniel were out there getting it on, for all I know." Something occurred to him and he tapped the table. "Mary is dead, by the way. Stroke. Happened yesterday. Could be you already knew that, but I doubt it. You've had other things on your mind."

RILEY LEFT HIM AT THE diner.

She drove north, out to Evenware Road, and pulled into the driveway of the house Mary had called home

125

for as long as Riley could remember. It appeared as solemn and quiet as a dead woman's residence should. But Riley knew Mary's son had been living with her for many years, and a vehicle—a red Corolla—that she assumed was his was parked in the carport.

Riley parked right behind the Corolla, went to the front door, and was surprised when it opened after only one ring of the doorbell.

The man before her was tall and awkward, and he knew who she was.

"Miss Constable," he said.

"Are you Lewis Evenware?"

"Yes ma'am."

"I'm sorry about your mom," Riley said, "and I know you don't really know me, but I was hoping we could talk."

"About what?"

Riley had of course expected questions, and in the calmest, most reassuring tone she could muster, she told him simply, "Current events."

Lewis's gaze was thick, but he stepped out of the way and ushered her in.

He shut the door behind her and led her through a single opening into a cramped, gray den with an empty wheelchair by the window.

No pleasantries, no offers of drinks or snacks. Lewis simply sat down on the couch and waited for Riley to do the same.

Riley sat down in an armchair to his left, and she noticed an opened suitcase on the couch next to her host. It was partially filled with clothes and toiletries.

126

"I'm leaving for now," Lewis said. "Why are you here, Constable?"

"You know there's been a lot going on."

"Yes."

"Could there be a connection to your family's old house? Nathaniel Golding was out there. Dean Mitchell is the one who found him. Now Dean is missing and…"

"Vacant old houses in the middle of nowhere are great places to do bad things."

"I agree. But is there more?"

"Like what?"

"Didn't your mom want to tear it down?"

"My mother was a good lady."

"I don't doubt that at all."

"You're not trying to draw some absurd connection between my mother—or me—and these dead people, are you?"

"No," she said, but God only knew how true it was.

"I can't help you, I'm sorry. I was young when I lived there. I've heard nothing about the place. Mother wanted it gone, yes. She said it was dangerous."

"When did she decide that?" Riley said.

For a long moment, Lewis just looked at her. "Last November. Fourteenth. I remember the night well, because she walked down there and stayed for a long time. I was worried about her. She forbade me to follow her."

"Did she walk down there a lot?"

"No. But it wasn't unheard of."

"What did she say when she got back?"

127

He stared at her again. "Nothing, Constable. But after that is when I first heard she wanted it torn down." He stopped, took a deep breath. "That's also when she started losing her mind."

Riley nodded at a picture on the wall, an old photo of Mary and the long gone man who Riley assumed was Lewis's dad.

"Was his name John?" Riley said.

"I don't know anything about him." Lewis's tone was unexpectedly sharp. "I don't want to."

21

THE CAFE WAS ON A mountaintop northwest of Little Rock, and if you sat out on the patio, you'd see to the east the city and all its lights and bridges and its reflection in the river, and to the west, the foothills of the Ouachita Mountains. Dean called this place "a magnificent secret." It all came together just right. If you came here on a pleasant autumn night, the city lights didn't interfere with the stars, and it was all reflected in the river, with the mountains sitting out there rolling and lonely, watching everything. Katelyn had accused him of being melodramatic, a wannabe romantic, something. You're too obvious, Dean Mitchell. Try again.

But he hadn't *totally* exaggerated. The views were nice. The patio setting was like something out of a Hemingway novel, lit by strands of bare bulbs hung around the perimeter. Nice effect. And the food was nice, too. Good enough. Much like their first date, generally. Nothing extravagant. But good enough.

"Are you okay?" he said.

He said this frequently for no reason at all. It was maddening.

She said she was fine. Quit asking her that.

So he asked her if she wanted more to drink.

"I better not."

"This place is something else, isn't it?"

"Just like you promised."

"Something else, Katelyn."

"What?"

Or was he simply repeating his sentiments about the cafe?

"Something else."

She'd been poking at one last bite of pasta, but now she set down her fork. "I don't know what you're talking about."

This was not their first date, she decided. If it had been, it wasn't anymore.

"You do know, don't you?" He pointed toward the city. "Look there."

She looked and saw the moon rising between two of Little Rock's high-rises. If it was not full, it was extremely close and would be tomorrow night. But, full or not, the fat silver of the moon amidst the city's electric blue was yet another magical aspect of the night. This was indeed *something else*.

For some reason, she thought his desire for her to notice the moon was the sweetest thing in the world, until she turned back to him and saw that he, too, was something else. Still a man. Still more or less Dean

Mitchell, but a macabre and still-shifting image of him. Specifically, a sizable wedge of his face beneath his right eye was gone, and a substance that she could only think of as tar was seeping out of his hair and down his face. She could not discern the source of the substance until she saw two new, pointed ears emerging from his skull.

Yellow cataracts coated his eyes. He tried to talk to her, but his mouth was incapable of speech. Yet he *did* talk to her. Something emerged from his mouth about the time his human ears began to dry and shrivel and sink into the sides of his head. This *something* that he said went straight to her mind—or was she insane?

I don't do well the night before. It hurts worse than that bullet I took in the face—at least that is healing now. Can you tell? Have you ever taken a bullet to the face, babe? No. No. Where did our first date go? Where did the years go? How about our lives? Remember me. Remember how badly this hurts.

He—it—tried to smile. It leaned into the table like it wanted to kiss her. She could smell its warm breath.

Some call it folklore. I call it hunger.

It reached for her. Reached out and touched her face, and for the first time since their first date ended and the moon rose, they weren't alone. There were others on the patio, ghostly strangers that weren't actually there, because you can't dream about strangers, but since they *were* there, why weren't they helping her? They were watching! Just watching!

It brought its fingertips down her face and wrapped those fingers around her throat, and it leaned so close that the remnants of its nose touched hers. *You know, and you won't admit it. Look at me. Take it in.*

131

She wanted to fight and scream, but she instead closed her eyes and recalled every foul thought and memory she had of him. It was a deafening explosion, right in the front of her brain, that took her out of this moment, wherever it was, *whenever* it was....

She opened her eyes.

To the present. She was upstairs with her guitars. She did not remember coming up here, but that was not surprising—what *could* she remember right now?

Oblivious, but not totally. She was awake, she knew where she was... and she knew something was wrong when she felt the sharp, cold touch of a breeze and saw that the octagon-shaped window at the end of the room was pushed open. It hadn't properly latched in years, but neither she nor Dean had ever thought about fixing it.

Dean was now in the room with her. Not the monstrous, rotting, sub-human thing from her dream, but her husband.

Almost.

Dean, yes, but not quite the Dean she'd married. The man sitting to her left on top of her Line 6 amplifier was more like her husband's psychotic identical twin. And there was a sinister aspect to him, too, a faint presence in the lines at the corners of his eyes and mouth.

She was scared, she admitted. But she was glad, too! She needed to talk to him. She had things to say, questions to ask.

"Let me tell you, Katelyn," Dean said. "There is a part of me that can't stand the thought of hurting you. But it won't always be. Kill me, or be killed."

132

He touched her like he loved her.
Then stood and walked over to the window.
By the time she wiped her eyes, he was gone.

22

RILEY STOPPED BY KATELYN'S HOUSE after she left
Lewis Evenware's company. She sat in the kitchen with
Katelyn and Robert and listened to Katelyn explain that
she didn't *know* that Dean Mitchell had been in the
house last night or this morning… it could've been a
dream. Robert had slept on the couch. Katelyn had tried
the bedroom, but she'd gone upstairs at some point,
unable to sleep and wanting to strum a guitar. Riley
listened, then went outside and circled around to the
house's east end, where the octagon window was indeed
pushed open. And yes, for the adequately agile, there
was a feasible path up there that involved the air
conditioning unit, a downstairs window, and a ledge in
the brickwork.

When Riley returned to her friends in the kitchen,
she said: "I'll try to talk to Palmer again. He might not
believe in monsters, but he believes in creeps."

If there was a difference.

RILEY WANTED TO BACKTRACK WITH Palmer and try again with softer rhetoric. Remind him that she understood his sentiments; she wasn't sure what she believed, either. Yes, of course, there was a certain narrative that was extremely hard to believe—and she didn't expect him to believe it! All of which was true, more or less.

But *she* believed it.

The thing in her headlights.

And *November 14th*, Lewis Eveware had said. The night Mary decided the house had to go. The full moon theme continued.

Not right now, she thought. *Backtrack.*

She tried to call Palmer, but he didn't answer. So she drove to his office in Harrison. If she didn't talk to him, that would be okay, for now. But Riley was going to make an effort. He'd been an ass this morning, but wasn't that a little bit forgivable?

When she reached the office, she was greeted by a deputy who informed her that Sheriff Palmer was not around at the present, and even if he was, based on what the deputy had heard, he wouldn't be interested in speaking to her.

Riley told the deputy to please have the sheriff call her, and she walked back outside to her vehicle.

SHE WAS GETTING INTO HER Jeep when a red Corolla drove by. She paused and stepped back out, wondering if it had been Lewis Evenware. As if to sate her curiosity, the driver turned around and pulled into the parking space beside her.

Lewis Evenware lowered the window and said: "I apologize for being difficult. I'm leaving for now. May I have your cell phone number?"

Riley gave it to him, hoping he would explain himself.

"I might be back," he said, before backing out and continuing on his way.

Riley watched his car until the road led him over a rise and out of sight.

Leaving for now… might be back…

She attempted to study his words, but he hadn't given her a lot to work with.

The iMessage came while Riley was turning onto the highway. She did not recognize the number, but she knew it was from Lewis; he'd waited till he was out of reach.

She swiped the screen to open the message. There was no text, simply a picture she assumed had been taken with his phone's camera. It was a sheet of notebook paper bearing the words "thomas wolf" in jagged, labored handwriting.

Now, Riley thought, setting the phone down and focusing on the road, *this is something to dive into.*

She hoped.

23

ROBERT INTENDED TO FINISH WHAT he'd started last night. It wouldn't take long, he told Katelyn, and he'd bring lunch back when he was done.

He returned to the unnamed remains of a dirt road and parked more or less in last night's parking spot. The whole scene looked radically different under the bright blue morning sky, everything out in the open and professing its innocence.

He collected his .30-06 from behind the seat, stuffed a bottle of water into his jacket's inside pocket, and set out north, toward the end of the road. He reached the drop-off where the road faded and cautiously descended the slope, digging his feet into the dirt and clinging tightly to trees, shrubs, and rocks. At the bottom, he sat down on a massive boulder on the creek's south bank and took a few sips of water.

He hadn't made it last night, but he was here now.

So what is it, you old fool? What's been gnawing at you?

Palmer and his minions had searched here. They'd followed the creek all the way to Elmer Kopps's place.

It was the land *beyond* Kopps's property that was at issue.

Robert suspected (no, *knew*) they'd kept following the creek. It was the most natural trail, after all, and it was the trail that had led them to Kopps's body.

But he had something else in mind.

He did not look around Kopps's property once he reached it. He was not down here to nose around and disregard yellow tape. No, he continued up the creek.

Years and years of maps came to him at once, and *now* he knew why he was out here.

Two or three hundred yards from Kopps's place, the steep incline to his left tapered substantially to a much gentler slope; the woods grew thick again, and just up ahead, the creek swung widely toward the northeast.

Robert followed it till he was in the center of the bend.

He felt so incredibly *alone*, he suddenly thought, though he really wasn't. He could still move anywhere toward the left and hit the highway again in less than twenty minutes. Behind him was Kopps's property, almost out of sight… and fifteen or so minutes from *that* was the ranger station. No, he wasn't *really* alone, but this low and lonely spot at least suggested solitude.

It feels lonely because it is.

Nobody comes here.

Which was the point. That was the spark that drove him out here and sent his memory—finally—to the maps.

Nobody came out here. And for the rare wanderer (or deputy) who did, he or she would inevitably be drawn to and along the creek. The rest was wilderness!

BUT HAD HE SEEN ON one of those old topographic maps a very faint red line branching away from the creek, somewhere in this bend? A red line that made an arching swoop to the southwest, toward and eventually along the base of Harrelston Ridge? That's exactly what he'd seen. But trails have a way of dying when they're not used and maintained, and Robert assumed that's what'd happened to this one. Certainly, it was not marked on the modern maps. And there was no sign of it here.

He left the creek and started west across a swath of knee-high brown grass, toward the edge of the woods. If it had been here, and if by chance his developing theory was correct, surely at least *some* trace of the path remained. But it might take a minute. And some bushwhacking.

He was right. He crossed the grass and proceeded up and down the edge of the woods for God knows how long, till at last he noticed an oh-so-faint corridor amidst the trees, where the brush was thinner and more beaten. The pathway into the trees was neither obvious nor obscure. It simply *was,* and if you weren't looking for it, you'd never notice it. Certainly not from the creek.

He took a few steps down the path and paused to orient himself. Where, exactly, would this take him? He was sure he remembered that faint red line following the ridge; that image was now ingrained in his head, and he was convinced it was real. But he couldn't pinpoint where the line had ended. Perhaps it had gone off into the indefinite region beyond the edge of the paper. How far did he intend to go?

If his memory of the map was indeed correct—and it had been thus far, right?—then this trail would cut a trek of approximately half a mile toward the Harrelston Bayou. Then, it would turn left and generally follow the bayou along the base of the ridge. Which meant...

Which meant he needed to just *go*. Standing here was accomplishing nothing.

THE TRAIL WAS INTERMITTENT.

Fairly clear followed by difficult to find, which became impossible; yet every time he thought he'd lost it and would have to revert to his age-rotted sense of direction to get him out of these woods, it returned. This went on for what felt like *much* more than half a mile, but eventually the trail led him to the east bank of the Harrelston Bayou, where, it made a sharp left and started south, eventually veering far enough away from the water that he lost sight of it. The woods thickened. And the trail, shortly after leaving the water, deteriorated again into near nonexistence.

How far am I willing to go? I'm not young anymore. No, that's bullshit. I'm old as hell. How far should I go?

But he pressed on.

Only stopping when, for no reason at all, the temperature dropped substantially.

140

He was in a low place where a narrow stream crossed the trail, undoubtedly on its way to the bayou. Everything was as it should be, except he was suddenly freezing despite his wool socks and Carhartt jacket. There was no breeze. There'd never been one.

At once, the reality of the situation came to him: he was deep in the woods, in a place he'd never been before, over a mile from his truck, and some devil (human variety or not) had killed out here and was likely *still* out here.

Was this why he felt so cold? Or was this deep chill something else… something external?

He was sure it was the latter. And the marks on a nearby tree confirmed it. One on top of the other, on top of the other, bark stripped away. He knew what they were, though he wished he didn't. *Do you want to see, Robert? Do you want me to show you?* The cold held him tighter. He heard a scream that was neither distant nor real. The cold crept deeper, and he saw a black spot just beyond the stream.

He stepped over the water and ascended a few feet to the point where the ground had obviously been disrupted. The black spot, he noticed, hunkering down with a wince and a grunt, was a Patagonia ball cap. It was both filthy and familiar to him. Marion Golding had worn it often.

Robert let himself fall back on his butt. He sat and looked at the hat and finally pulled out his phone and took three pictures of it, reaching out in several directions to capture different angles. Then he grabbed hold of a tree and pulled himself to his feet. Stepped back. Took several pictures of the area.

Service out here was bad, but his phone showed two bars.

He almost called Riley, then decided to wait. The hat had waited for a month or more. It could wait another hour. There was at least one more puzzle piece left to find.

He continued on.

Half an hour later, he arrived at a crossroads of a much clearer (though not regularly maintained) east-west trail. This, Robert knew immediately, was the trail to the Harrelston Lookout. He could make a right here, cross the bayou on a log bridge, and start a winding course up the face of the ridge. Or he could turn left and return to town; he'd eventually hit the dead end of Spruce Street.

Obviously, there was no reason to do either of these. But he was glad to know his exact location. And if he'd already reached the Harrelston Lookout intersection…

After another quarter of a mile, the trail cut gently away from the bayou, toward the southeast, and finally disappeared altogether at the edge of a clearing. The open space was covered in dirt and rocks and patches of dormant knee-high grass. And on its opposite side was the sight that Robert had expected to see: the back of the rotting hulk that was the Evenware House.

Connection made.

24

KATELYN WAS PUTTING A FOURTH and final wood screw in the upstairs octagon window when Riley called to tell her that she was on her way to meet Robert near the ranger station. He'd found a path that led all the way to the Evenware House. Furthermore, he was sure he'd found where Marion Golding died.

"Maybe there will be some trace of your husband, too," Riley said.

"I'll help." Katelyn finished off the final screw and set down the drill. "Should I meet you at the station?"

"If you're willing, there's actually something else I'd like you to do," Riley said. "Start digging into the Evenware family. I'll send you a text that might give you a starting point."

Katelyn was intrigued and not at all disappointed. Playing Nancy Drew didn't sound half bad, much better than stomping fruitlessly through the woods all afternoon.

"Sure," Katelyn said. "Okay."

A few seconds after she ended the call, her phone dinged.

THE MESSAGE READ, "WRITTEN BY Mary Evenware?" and included a picture of a handwritten note: thomas wolf.

Now Katelyn was intrigued.

Thomas Wolf. *Thomas* was a name, obviously. But what about *Wolf?* Had she been in the midst of a final delusion and misspelled the name of a random writer? Or was that second word *not* a name at all?

It was definitely time to play detective.

SHE DROVE TO THE COURTHOUSE in Harrison and found her way to the dreary (and thankfully empty) chamber containing rows and stacks of land records. Thankfully, most of it was accessible via a desktop computer in the corner of the room. She sat down in front of the computer, lightly drummed her fingers along the keys as she thought, and dove in with a search for THOMAS WOLF. The search was as fruitless as she'd expected it to be. Next, she keyed in THOMAS EVENWARE. *This* conjured up many results... all for the name Evenware, none of which were named Thomas.

Still, she clicked on the first document, a warranty deed from 1937: Edmund Pike deeding to Grady and Carrie Evenware a piece of property "containing ten acres, more or less" just east of Harrelston Bayou.

Further up the list she found a deed from March of 1977 quitclaiming the same ten acres from Grady to John and Mary Evenware.

Katelyn printed both of these and kept digging.

The last item of interest was a deed from 1990, with only Mary Evenware's name on it. Four acres of property on Evenware Road. This was the property Mary had now—or, rather, the property on which she'd just died.

Katelyn printed this one as well and stepped over to the clerk's office to pay for the pages.

HALF AN HOUR LATER, SHE was at her breakfast table with her laptop and a glass of iced tea. Bright sunshine poured through the window over the sink.

She fed Google the name EVENWARE and received over twelve-thousand hits, none of which—based off her perusal of the first ten pages of results—were about the family from northern Arkansas.

A search for THOMAS WOLF, despite the spelling, would bring up tons of information about the author and Katelyn doubted "wolf" in Mary's last message should be interpreted as a name, anyway. So she tried THOMAS EVENWARE. And here was a man with that name; he was from Minnesota, and he apparently hadn't used his Twitter account in over a year. This individual, obviously, was not who she was looking for.

She reached into her jacket, which was tossed over the back of her chair, and retrieved the printouts from the courthouse.

She keyed into Google the first name she saw: GRADY EVENWARE. This search was more productive. At the top of the first page of results was Grady Evenware's obituary from the *Sun Gazette*. Katelyn clicked it and learned that Grady, born in 1915, had died in 1978. He was preceded by his wife, Carrie, and survived by his only son, Jonathon.

Katelyn opened a blank Word document and copied and pasted the obituary's text into it. Then, she moved to the next and only other relevant item in Google's list: a photo of Grady's grave marker on a website simply called *Cemeteries of Arkansas*. The marker was interesting but she didn't see how it was helpful.

She then typed in JONATHON EVENWARE, and to filter out some of the excess, she added ELLINGWOOD, AR next to his name. Searched.

Nothing. No obituary. No grave marker. No teases for information from any of the many family history websites. Truly, nothing.

"Damn," Katelyn said.

For a few minutes, she sat and drank her tea, until an idea dawned, and she leaned forward and searched GRADY EVENWARE ANCESTORS. This produced a few substantial results. She clicked through various sites for twenty or thirty minutes and decided to follow what looked like a promising trail at a website called *My Family History*. It promised access to records and, potentially, construction of a family tree.

"We'll see, won't we?" Katelyn said, and fed the site Grady's name.

The site did its work, and Katelyn dug.

An hour later, she didn't have much, but she did have *some*, including a birth record that revealed that Grady Evenware had been born in a town called Idalia, Maryland. She also had deeds, the most interesting of which was a 1927 executor's deed passing property to a Maxwell Evenware from the deceased *Thomas Evenware*.

Now she needed *facts* to go with these names and dates.

She copied and pasted the information from the family history website into the Word document she'd created earlier. This done, she opened a new tab in the web browser, searched IDALIA, MD., and learned that it was a map dot with 442 inhabitants, on the Chesapeake Bay side of Maryland's Eastern Shore.

1927, she thought.

Time for a new search.

Into the Google search bar she typed: THOMAS EVENWARE IDALIA, MD 1927.

A few minutes later, she thought she might go to Maryland.

25

FOR THE SECOND TIME IN the last month, Riley sat on the edge of a rock outcropping near the top of Harrelston Ridge. It was a cold and gloomy day, and she was alone. In all directions, endless miles of forests and hills. Due east was Ellingwood's insignificant cluster of old buildings and side streets. Directly below her, somewhere in that brown forest, was the Evenware House.

It was Friday. She'd come up here at first to look around, then to think, to convince herself she was still sane, that the fog in her brain had not totally consumed her. Because the last few days had been both stressful and uneventful. She remembered everything, yet she could point to very few specifics. She recalled Katelyn calling her on Wednesday to tell her she was leaving for Maryland and would not be gone long.

Yes, Riley remembered *that*. But beyond *that*, her memories of the prior three days were a conglomeration of her sitting in the cafe, sitting at home, looking at the computer, looking at her phone, reading, staring at the television, trying to distract herself, driving, searching, and finding nothing. Her life had been consumed by an absurd trinity: Dean Mitchell, the Evenware House, and the moon. This trinity had fogged her mind and days, and Riley wondered how much the *fog* was responsible for what she'd seen—or thought she'd seen—this morning.

She'd parked in front of the Evenware House, intending to search the property for the first time since Robert's discovery of Marion's hat. But she never went in the house, because of the man peering at her through the broken grime of the front window. *Not a man. A black-and-white* memory *of a man.*

So she'd started walking, at first aimlessly, then with purpose, needing to process the dead man in the window.

Throughout her childhood and early adulthood, Riley had never believed in anything that was not part of the physical, rational world. She once informed a high school English teacher that, if forced to say, she was definitely a student of the Enlightenment, *not* of the transcendentalists. She barely knew what she was talking about, but the underlying point was more than true, and it followed her into adulthood. *Maybe* this rational, reasonable, give-me-just-the-facts view of the world started changing a few years ago, when she read a novel called *The Little Stranger*, by Sarah Waters. At the time, the book was well outside the boundaries of her typical reading habits… but she read it on a whim, and the book unnerved her for days.

Why? She was a rational person! She was a student of *reason*!

Maybe it was the book's subtlety, its slow-burn approach.

Maybe that's when and how her mind began to change. Or expand.

Her phone sounded from the depths of her jacket.

Sheriff Palmer, she saw, once she'd retrieved it.

"It's been a while," she answered.

"I guess so," Palmer said, "but we never had the most regular line of communication to start with. Anyway, I have an update for you."

"Okay."

"Quick response time on those prints we lifted from Elmer's trailer. They're Dean Mitchell's. One was just damned near perfect, left on the glass in the back door for the world to see. So the missing lawyer is officially the most important character in our narrative."

"I've been after him for a week."

"Let's work together on finding this guy, Riley. I *want* to work together. What I don't want is a fantasy."

Silence. Riley wasn't stunned, excited, upset, or anything else. She simply had nothing to say.

"Are you with me?" Palmer said.

Riley stared out over the forest. She locked her eyes on her not-so-distant community and wondered how dangerous things really were.

"Are you with *me*?" she said.

"On the importance of finding this lunatic lawyer? Sure thing. I hope that's enough."

26

BASED OFF THE INFORMATION SHE'D found online and in the county phone book, there was an Evenware remaining in Idalia, Maryland: an old woman named Paula. This was (unless *My Family History* was wrong) Jonathon Evenware's cousin... and Thomas's great-granddaughter. Katelyn thought it made sense to begin the next stage of her *Nancy Drew* game by speaking to Paula Evenware, and it was probably best to do so in person.

And so, after checking into a local establishment called the Apple Tree Inn and taking a much-needed power nap, Katelyn set out into town.

First, a late supper at a sandwich shop near the motel. Then, she keyed Paula's address into Apple Maps. Two miles, the app said, and the route looked easy enough: down this road for a little over half a mile, then left.

Katelyn pulled out of the sandwich shop's lot and started along the course.

The route was not as easy as it looked.

After the left turn, the *street* turned into a narrow one-lane gravel road that cut through the bottom of a forested canyon north of town. This *had* to be wrong, Katelyn thought. But almost two miles from the sandwich shop, the canyon walls faded away, and she found herself pulling into the driveway of a very old but seemingly well-kept little house that had likely once been the centerpiece of a farm.

Katelyn parked and approached the door and rang the bell.

The old woman who answered was, according to the birthdate provided by *My Family History*, almost eighty-five, but she acted and sounded like one at least fifteen years younger—one for whom honest-to-God *old age* was a new idea not yet accepted. The old woman smiled and said hello and asked what she could do for her. Katelyn, not wanting to give everything away from the front stoop, simply said she'd come all the way from Arkansas and wondered if they could talk, just for a moment.

Paula's expression shifted—a mere flicker of unease—but she showed her in.

"It's warmed up a little bit, believe it or not," Paula said, leading Katelyn through a house that was impressively neat while still very much lived in. "I am so very ready for spring."

The den in which they settled featured a flat-panel television and satellite box. A John Grisham paperback was broken open on the arm of Paula's chair. All things considered, Katelyn thought, this old lady was doing well for herself.

"Do you want a drink, Mrs. Mitchell?" Paula Evenware said. "I don't remember if I asked already."

Katelyn declined the offer, and the old woman asked what it was that had brought her all the way from Arkansas to Maryland.

"Family, I assume," Paula said. "I know most of us Evenwares are down that way, what few are left."

Here it is, Katelyn thought. *This is where I speak. Did I expect it to be easier? Maybe I expected somebody senile. That would be easier, wouldn't it?*

"I'm from Ellingwood, where Jonathon and his wife are from."

Paula nodded. "John is my cousin. A shame. I don't even know what became of him. I haven't heard from John since... forever."

"So you don't know what happened to him?"

"What did happen?"

"I don't think anybody knows. I thought you might have heard, somehow."

Paula shook her head and said she was very sorry. But there *was* something on her face, or perhaps behind her eyes, that suggested this topic had triggered a memory, a thought, something.

Katelyn didn't press it.

"Do you know anything about a Thomas Evenware?"

"My great-grandfather." Paula's head tilted a bit as she thought. "Died a long, long time ago. His parents came here from England. That's where we are all from. Did somebody ask about him?"

153

"Something like that," Katelyn said.

"What would you like to know? I can't say I'm full of knowledge about him. He died so long ago, before I was born."

"Was he from here?" Katelyn said.

"He was born in a little church, actually, just south of here, along the coast. 1868, it was. Mother went into labor during the preaching, they say. New Harbor Church. I don't even know if it's still there. It was as of ten or twenty years ago. Born there, buried there. He just loved that church, supposedly, and they thought it would save his eternal soul. It would be sweet, I suppose."

"Would be?"

"He died fairly young, and unnaturally, in 1927. So I can't say the story is *sweet*."

"How did he die?"

"He was *killed*. We Idalia folks have known it for many years. At least the Evenwares, though I'm the only one left. He was not sick, he was killed, right in the middle of what is now Paris Street, behind the music store."

Katelyn had intended to avoid taking notes. But she typed this information into the notepad app on her phone.

Paula noticed and did not seem to mind.

"Why?" Katelyn said.

"Local lore says he killed people. What *local lore* we have. Idalia once had a few thousand people. We're down to less than 500 and shrinking. Most here are oblivious. But *I've* always heard they executed him, shot him in the street. Any newspaper actually saying this is

154

long gone or never existed. I never researched the matter, true. But my mother did. Not that there was anything to research. Just tales, passed down and passed down."

"There is no documentation at all? Nothing?"

"No articles. No photographs. Just folklore." The old woman paused, thought for a moment. "But there *is* something you might be interested in."

PAULA RECOMMENDED SHE GO TO the library, but the library was closed by the time she left her house.

And so, after returning to town, she found the location Paula had referenced: Paris Street, behind the music store. It was in the center of what little downtown Idalia had.

Katelyn pulled her Kia rental into a nearby parking lot and thought: *Right here. Almost a century ago. Right here, what happened? Death, nothing, some significant thing. Totally unrelated to my concerns? Or right at the heart of it?*

IT SHOULD HAVE BEEN A night of deep, hard-earned sleep. Lord, she was tired enough for it.

Instead, it was hours of staring at the ceiling, bathroom light on because she was, for the first time in her life, afraid of the dark... especially the thick, stinking darkness of a small town seedy motel room.

At ten 'o clock, she got a message from Robert: *How are you?*

She replied: *I'm okay. Can't sleep.*

Same, he said.

155

She thought he might ask what she was doing, what she'd found. Something.

But no. And that was that.

SHE FELL ASLEEP SOMETIME AFTER four a.m., awoke at eight, let herself doze for another hour, then got up and got ready and drove down to the one story stone building that was the Idalia Public Library.

A fifty-something woman with the face of a deflated basketball was behind the counter to the right of the door. She was flicking at her phone and did not look up as Katelyn walked in.

A few sad rows of books stood to her left. And straight ahead, just as Paula had mentioned as she handed Katelyn her purse ("Don't forget this! Oh, and when you go in the library tomorrow…"), was the "Media Room."

It was a cramped, dim chamber that contained three computers, one to the left of the door and two along the wall across from it.

Katelyn could not care less about the computers. Concerning her Evenware research, she'd milked modern technology for all it had to offer, at least to the best of her abilities.

She was interested in the framed artwork on the walls above the monitors. Particularly the one to the left.

Paula had said it would be on point, and it was.

It appeared to be a reproduction of a pencil and ink drawing, a black and gray nightmare of slashes, swirls, and smudges… depicting the scene Paula had described yesterday. There was Paris Street. There, too, was the back of the building that was now a music store. There was the familiar, inhuman thing lurched over in the middle of the street, tall and lanky, splotched with fur, canine ears. And there was a man, near the edge of the sketch, with a gun extended before him. A crowd lurked in the background, faint gray smudges with ghostly, gasping faces.

The picture was at the center of a small, yellowed sheet of paper that had obviously once been in a book. In the top right corner was the page number—112— and below the illustration was the caption "Fig. 21: Idalia, Maryland."

She used her phone to take a picture of the page, then leaned in to study the thing at the center of the sketch.

"Need something?" A woman's voice, from behind her. "Or are you just enjoying our art museum?"

Katelyn turned and found herself mere feet from the deflated basketball. The librarian stood just inside the media room's door, one hand on her hip, the other wrapped around her phone.

"I'm curious about this picture." Katelyn searched for something else. "Do you know what book it's from?"

"Nope. They just found that page tucked in some dead Evenware's house, so the story goes. Are you fond of morbid things like that?"

"No. I was just curious."

"I was thinking maybe you'd want to use a computer. I don't have any idea about that thing, just like I don't know why they want it hanging there. But that's where it's been since I can remember."

A SEARCH FOR "NEW HARBOR Church" did not yield any map results, and so she pulled into a gas station south of town, bought a bottle of water, and asked the woman behind the counter if she knew where it was.

The woman drummed her fingers on the counter as she animatedly contorted her face to signify her thinking.

"I assume that's probably the little church just down the road there. Nothing much there now." The attendant nodded and pointed out the door, past a stranger who'd just come in and was staring hard, for some reason, at Katelyn. "So when you leave here, go right, and keep going south. A few miles south of here, there's a Y. Go left and you stay on the highway. Go right and it kind of goes down toward the water. Go right. There's a little old church down there that hasn't been used for a long time. That's all I can think of."

Katelyn thanked her and left, stepping lightly past the staring stranger.

The attendant was right.

The church sat about a hundred feet up the slope from the bay. The building was smaller than most one-room schoolhouses, a gray, dilapidated thing that would likely be finished off by the next blast of severe weather.

In faded paint above the doors were the words NEW HARBOR CHURCH.

Katelyn parked amidst some weeds near the front of the building and did not spend long inside the church. It contained nothing but the remnants of things gone.

She found what she was looking for down the slope and to the right of the building, marked by a stone that was barely readable; only a few letters of his last name were still legible. But it wasn't the stone that drew her attention. It was the plant that grew over his grave, several feet tall and bright green, adorned beautifully with light purple flowers.

Despite the cold gray of the current season.

27

ROBERT WAS ATTEMPTING TO CARE about the day's newspaper when Riley called and asked if he'd like to meet her at The Painted Lady.

He told her he'd be there in ten minutes.

They sat in a corner near the bathrooms, as far away from the other patrons as they could get. After they ordered, Riley took out her phone, pressed something, and handed it to him.

He took it and saw a photo of a drawing. Out of an old book, it looked like. Pencil, ink, both? The drawing depicted something skinny and partially covered in fur, at least half animal, hunched over in pain as a faceless somebody fired at it from behind.

Robert took it in, set the phone down, and waited for Riley to explain.

"Katelyn sent me that," she said.

The waiter brought their drinks: sweet tea for Riley, water for Robert.

"When will she get back?" he said. "Maryland, right?"

"She's flying into Little Rock tomorrow."

"Tell me about the picture."

"She said it's hanging in the local library. She can't find anybody who knows who drew it, or what book it's from, but the only Evenware left in town thinks it depicts how a guy named Thomas Evenware died. Mary left that final message, 'Thomas wolf,' and I think this Thomas looks pretty familiar, don't you?"

"Unfortunately."

"Thomas Evenware is John's—Mary's husband who disappeared—great-grandfather. And if you'll remember, John is the one who moved down here and built the Evenware House."

"So it runs in the family."

"That seems to be it."

"What about Dean Mitchell? He's not in the family."

The waiter brought their food.

A minute or two of relative silence passed as they began to eat.

"But there is an obvious connection between Dean Mitchell and the Evenwares," Riley said.

"The house. Do you think it's something to do with John? Nobody ever figured out what happened to him."

Riley stared at her sandwich as if it featured some mystical inscription.

"Maybe he's still out there," she said.

THEY DROVE OUT TO THE Evenware House in Riley's Jeep.

As she drove, Riley told him what she'd seen in one of the house's front windows. It had, she said, looked like an old man.

"You think you saw his ghost?"

"I don't know."

It was nearly dark by the time Riley pulled to the side of the driveway. She retrieved a flashlight from the glove compartment and flipped the safety on her gun. Robert followed her across the wasteland of a lawn, through what was left of the front door, and into the dusty darkness beyond it.

The place was rank.

There was a plant growing tall in the far corner, right out of the cracks in the floorboards. It was springtime green, absurd, and drawing them closer.

"You'll be the first to go, you bitch."

The words were spoken by a dry, male voice, and Robert shook his head vehemently when Constable Riley turned around to see if *he'd* said it—not that it *could've* been him; the words had come from a distant part of the house.

"Dean?" Riley aimed the flashlight toward the stairs. "John? Who's there?"

I don't think I want to know, Robert thought. *'You'll be the first to go, you bitch.' Point taken.*

"You heard it, right?" Riley said to him.

"I heard it."

162

Robert's heart was racing. He didn't want to be here.

Out of the distant darkness—from the plant?—came another noise. A creaking board.

Riley raised the gun and aimed the flashlight toward the plant.

Robert yearned for his rifle, though if there *were* dead things here that were still speaking and moving around, bullets probably wouldn't be very effective.

The plant is moving.

"We're both thinking the same thing, aren't we?" Riley said.

"I think so."

She turned again and asked him to return to the Jeep with her.

RILEY OPENED THE JEEP'S REAR hatch and retrieved a black canvas tool bag from the cargo area. She withdrew from the bag a hammer and a flat pry bar and confirmed that Robert would rather pry up floorboards than shoot ghosts, and they returned to the deepest corner of the den.

They knelt near the plant, and Robert jammed the sharp end of the pry bar into the gap between two of the boards. Riley was directly across from him, flashlight in one hand, gun in the other.

Robert tapped the bar with the hammer and pushed downward, applying moderate pressure. Nothing, more pressure, still nothing... another tap from the hammer, more pressure, and, finally, the board moaned. Robert moved the bar down its length—the *ting* of the hammer on the bar, the screeching and moaning of the board and its nails—until he tossed the board aside and revealed a layer of rotted sub flooring that was easily knocked away with the clawed end of the hammer. When he was done, he'd formed a hole of approximately six inches by two feet that was crossed by two joists.

Riley aimed the flashlight beam into the pit and revealed a shadow so dark it shined.

Because it was not a shadow at all.

"Oh hell," Robert said.

The creature in the midst of Riley's flashlight beam was the biggest black widow spider Robert had ever seen. A braver fool than he could spin it for a hell of a curve ball.

The nasty thing reared itself up and seemed to lock its half dozen or so eyes on the bright light and the humans beyond it. Robert swore it made some kind of sound—a slight chirp, maybe, probably a taunt.

Riley was obviously thinking about shooting it, but Robert made the decision for her; he brought the sharp end of the pry bar down like a stake, and the monstrous spider *crunched* open and bled out onto the dirt.

Riley relaxed a bit and aimed the light deeper into the void under the floor.

Toward the far end of the hole was the fleshy base of the plant. Several of its lower branches extended toward them; many reached on into the darkness.

Robert used the end of the bar to scrape the spider's carcass out of the way, and when he did so, a foul odor—something close to rot, but somehow worse—wafted out of the dirt.

"What do you think?" Riley said.

Robert poked at the ground with the pry bar. "Did you bring a shovel?"

28

KATELYN WAS IN A HAZE when she walked off the plane in Little Rock at 10:40 p.m. She hadn't had a decent night's sleep in three days, and the three cocktails she'd had at Pittsburgh International were hanging with her still. She caught a ride in a shuttle that took her to her car, and for a long while she simply sat behind the Honda's wheel and looked at her phone, even though she wasn't looking at anything. Just thinking. Or maybe she wasn't doing that, either. How many hours home? Two, three? Two or three hours of winding, stomach churning, two-lane ribbon.

Tomorrow, she thought. So close yet so far. All that.

She drove to a nearby hotel and checked into a room and soon found herself sitting on the side of the bed in her jeans and bra, trying to find the motivation to move. She took an Advil and used the bathroom, took off her jeans, and crawled beneath the covers.

She realized as she fell asleep that she hadn't taken her phone out of airplane mode.

But that was okay.

SHE AWOKE THE NEXT MORNING at a few minutes past ten. She sat up and kicked her legs off the bed and decided she felt better. Not *great*—her head still hurt, just a little, and her stomach was mildly upset—but better. She picked up her phone and turned off airplane mode, and the device *dinged* and *ka-thunked* with a variety of incoming notifications.

She flipped through them as she stood in the bathroom brushing her teeth.

Two text messages. Riley asking how she was doing, an old college friend wondering if her husband did probate law.

She'd also accumulated two junk emails, one from Ticketmaster, one from an insurance company. And there was a third email that wasn't junk. It had been sent last night at 2:52 in the morning. The sender was DEAN, and there was no subject.

She tapped the message with her thumb.

It was very short: *You love old country songs.*

This was followed by two lines of text, both of which were obviously chord progressions... from her binder of songs:

Em   D   A   Em
Dm   C   G

Her emotions—in the span of about a minute—went from fear to confusion to a gut-sinking understanding.

167

"You psycho," she said.

RILEY ANSWERED HER CALL IMMEDIATELY, and the first thing she asked was if she was okay.

"I got a room in Little Rock and left my phone in airplane mode. I'm okay."

This wasn't entirely true. She was pacing the room in yesterday's underwear, and her head was pounding once again.

"You don't sound okay," Riley said. "Robert and I went to the Evenware House. Do you have a minute?"

"No. I think he might be in my house." She stopped and sat down on the side of the bed, wrapped her free arm around her stomach. "I got an email from Dean. He sent it last night at like two or three in the morning. It's guitar chords."

It took Riley a moment to respond. She was obviously confused.

"What does that mean?"

"It's two country songs I like to play. One song is called 'Past the Point of Rescue' and the other is 'Stranger in my House.' He's a psycho. It's pretty clear."

Silence. From both ends of the conversation.

"Call 911," Riley finally said. "I'm on my way."

KATELYN FELT BETTER AFTER SHE'D showered and put on fresh clothes.

Crying probably helped some, too.

She'd just zipped her suitcase and was cramming the bottle of Advil she'd nearly left on the bedside stand down into her purse… when she saw something *in* her purse that she knew did not belong to her. It was a folded over envelope, crammed into the bottom of her purse's side pocket, partially hidden beneath some tampons and a pack of gum.

It was obviously old, she thought as she withdrew it. The blue ink on it was faded and smudged.

It was addressed to Paula Evenware and was still sealed. Or *re*-sealed? She couldn't tell.

She did not have to wonder where it came from. Paula Evenware had obviously *placed it* in her purse.

Why'd she given it to her like this? Probably because she preferred to not relive certain memories.

JANUARY 12, 1990

Dear Paula,

My dad died almost twelve years ago, in 1978. He was your uncle, of course, and I know you barely knew him, but he was my FATHER, my EVENWARE, the only real blood I knew. He developed cancer and was not interested in "dragging things out." Time to accept things, he thought, and he wanted to deed his property to us and be done with it.

Before he stumbled and died (and that's exactly what happened, heart attack, caused by the disease?), he forced himself to take a slow and painful walk with me up to the Harrelston Bayou. You must crest a rise before you go down to the water, so we did not travel the whole distance. Just far enough. We sat down, and he said he accepted death. Not death generally (though that too), but THIS CERTAIN ONE. There is a physical corruption in our family, he said. Over sixty years, sanity intact, with an ailment as mundane as cancer? He said it wasn't bad at

169

all, really, and he'd take it gladly and be glad to see Mama again, because there is much worse in the Evenware blood. He said that Thomas Evenware was the last BAD CASE he knew of. But he told me that he wanted me to be aware. Why? There's a smell about you lately, John. *And that's all he said. I still don't know, Paula. I want to understand. What do you know about our ancestors? Why won't you talk to me? Will you write?*

When my dad told me there was a 'physical corruption' in our blood, when he told me there was a stench about me, even back then, in '78, even then, he knew it was in me. It was not immediately evident. It took years. I put my father in the ground feeling physically *okay. Mary and I moved into the house, and I felt okay while we moved. I did my best to shrug off what he said about my 'stench,' shoved it down, got over it. I grieved for my dad for I don't know how long. And I moved on with my life. Mary wanted a child, but it just wouldn't happen... Until it did. His name is Lewis. He was born in 1980. When I look at him, I'm concerned. Mary knows nothing about this. And I can't explain it.*

My first symptoms arrived in 1989. I guess I could call it insomnia. It was not severe, but it devastated my moods. And I only wish that was all. I noticed the first lump on Christmas Day, 1989. It was a soft marble on my left elbow. Painless. I wanted to believe it was some sort of inflammation, but I didn't. By New Year's Day, there was a golf ball on the back of my neck and a deep, throbbing, persistent pain in my lower back. How amusing! I'm stuffed full of disease! See you soon, Dad! Why not believe that? But it's totally wrong. Don't misunderstand—something is growing inside me. But this is nothing that can be diagnosed or treated by doctors. CORRUPTION, remember? Last night, the moon was almost full. The tingling hatred that palpably spread through me confirmed my thoughts. I tried to tell Mary why I

170

could not go to the doctor. She scoffed. She screamed at me. She told me she loved me and I WAS going to the doctor! Quit listening to whatever foolishness my dad put into my head. He's dead! She'd been angering me for sometime. Just her presence— and Lewis's. I was burning inside. Hell, festering in my body. Neither of them could possibly understand, yet they both remained, knowing nothing, casting their judgments and rendering their meaningless advice. Did Mary deserve what I eventually told her? You'll be the first to go, you bitch. *Did she deserve that? Did Lewis hear it?*

I hate what this is. I know it can be traced further back than Thomas. And I know it will somehow continue beyond me. Is it contagious? Does it matter? Do you feel it too?

I don't know what happens tonight at moonrise. I suspect it will at best be the beginning of my end. Be careful. Do what you can. Please write.

John Evenware
Ellingwood, Arkansas

29

RILEY WAS PARKED ON THE curb two houses down
from Katelyn's, checking her mirrors constantly for the
sheriff. Or for the husband.

Palmer arrived in a marked Explorer, and two
deputies were right behind him in a plain black Charger.

"Just get here?" Palmer asked as she approached
him.

"Just a minute ago."

Riley and the deputies followed the sheriff up the
yard and into the garage, which Riley opened with the
keypad code Katelyn had given her.

Palmer rang the bell and knocked. Then rang the
bell again.

After what was probably twenty or thirty seconds
with no answer, Palmer knocked one more time.

Nothing.

Palmer did his best to peer through the curtain over the door's window.

"Looks dark. I don't think anybody's here."

"He could be dead," Riley said.

Palmer muttered *Oh hell* and banged his fist on the door again. "Dean Mitchell?" he called through the glass. "Sheriff Palmer. Open up if you're in there, okay? Consider this a kind request and don't make me go beyond it."

Five seconds. Ten seconds. Nothing.

Palmer turned around and looked out over the yard. "Hal Ketchum and Ronnie Milsap? I miss that kind of country, but I could kick their asses."

He directed his deputies to the back of the house then turned and sent his right boot into the door, directly beneath the knob. There was a faint *crunch*, and two more kicks finished the job.

The door swung inward and bounced off the Mitchells' washing machine.

Riley and Palmer stepped over the threshold and did not turn on any lights as Palmer led the way through the laundry room and into a small corridor that split left into the kitchen and breakfast nook and right into the master bedroom. Palmer nodded at Riley to take the bedroom; he would search the kitchen area.

The bedroom looked exactly as it should: bed made, television off, a pile of change on the dresser, a neat stack of clothes on the treadmill in the corner. The door to the master bathroom was closed, however, and Riley found this strange. No reason, really, other than her (baseless?) belief that most people don't close their bathroom doors unless they're *using* the bathroom.

173

She drew her gun and approached the door. Opened it with her right hand, nudged it in… and her first impression was *nothing*. Just an empty bathroom. Now, he could be—

"Riley."

The voice came from the bathroom's shadowy depths. The shower? She flung back the curtain and found the shower empty. The voice came again, from behind her, and she scolded herself for her delusional paranoia as she turned around to face Palmer.

He put a finger over his lips and led her into the den… where both deputies were standing. They were looking toward the sectioned off area at the back of the room that contained the stairs. For a second, Riley thought they were looking *at* the stairs. But then the smell touched her nose, and she knew what they were thinking.

The door to the half bath next to the stairs was shut. There was no light spilling through the crack beneath it.

But the smell was unmistakable.

Palmer stepped up to the door and knocked lightly.

"Mr. Mitchell?"

No answer.

"Anybody in there?"

Palmer knocked again, then ran his hands along the top of the doorframe and found the emergency key. He used it to unlock the door, and the odor billowed out of the darkness, so thick it was almost visible.

Riley and the deputies hung back several feet.

Palmer put a hand on his nose, entered the reeking shadows, and told the unconscious figure on the toilet that he was under arrest for the murder of Elmer Kopps.

RILEY STEPPED OUT BACK AND inhaled the cold air; she tried to call Katelyn but was thankful when there was no answer. Another breath, this one much deeper. The stench that had poured out of the bathroom had been among the foulest odors she'd ever encountered. Nothing about it was normal or healthy. The sticky, tar-like mess splattered on both the toilet and the floor only reinforced the idea that something was physically— *badly*—wrong with Dean Mitchell.

But that was not news.

The screen door opened behind her.

"Care to come along?" Palmer said.

One last deep breath. "I'll follow you."

"YES, COFFEE." DEAN MITCHELL RAISED his cuffed hands and took the cup from Palmer.

The interview room in the sheriff's department smelled faintly of chemicals and was lit with a single-bulb fixture that hugged the ceiling directly above the folding table in the middle of the room. The poor lighting did strange things to Dean Mitchell's face, Riley thought. His permanent, insane snicker glowed ghost-like in the dim gray. For a man who'd just been caught in such a humiliating position, he radiated a tremendous arrogance.

"I'll talk all you want," Mitchell said, "even though I don't have to. But *just* to you two."

Palmer said: "I've been hearing some crazy stuff lately. I want explanations."

"You *think* you do."

"What happened to your face?"

"I think it was a .30-06. Ask Robert."

Palmer glanced quickly at Riley. "A .30-06 to the face, and you're sitting here talking to me. Explain that."

"There is nothing to explain. There are no answers. You think you have questions, but you're just hurling sand grains at a force of nature."

Riley's eyes widened.

"Good God, Dean," Palmer said. "Act like you know me. You do, right? Flatter me if I'm suddenly so unworthy of your company."

"That's why I'm here."

"You're here because I arrested you."

"You're right. And wrong."

"That's fair. You don't have to say a word. But since you said you would, answer my unworthy questions."

"You haven't learned the most important lesson there is: you don't know a fucking thing."

Palmer clicked his pen and tapped the legal pad in front of him. "Let's work backwards. Forget Elmer Kopps for now. Why were you in that house?"

"Because it's mine."

"Katelyn says you haven't been there since February... tenth, eleventh? That's what she told Constable Saunders. It's February twentieth, Dean. So yeah, that house is yours, but you haven't been acting like it. Why now?"

"Because it's mine."

"Where have you been?"

"The woods."

Palmer didn't push it. For now. "Did you come home to see your wife?"

"No."

"So what were you doing in there?"

"It's *evident*, isn't it?"

"Besides that."

"That's my house. Those are my things."

"You didn't go in there to make contact with your wife?"

"I knew she wasn't in there."

"'Kill me or be killed.' Did you ever say that or something like that to her?"

"Seems like it." A sip of coffee. "It's good advice."

From her spot on the wall, Riley said: "Can you just not be obnoxious?"

"Let me see." Dean Mitchell shifted in his seat and directed his gaze to the ceiling. "I believe I told that to my wife on February *twelfth*. What was the occasion?"

"Occasion?"

"What was the occasion? What was going on?"

Palmer clicked the pen a couple of times and lowered his head. "I don't like being quizzed."

"I'm not fucking quizzing you."

"It was the morning after the full moon." Riley's words were barely more than a whisper.

Dean Mitchell turned to her, grinning.

"And?" Palmer said.

The lawyer refocused on the man in front of him. "And so I was coming down from a traumatic high. Have you ever felt your flesh fusing back together,

177

Sheriff Palmer? Have you ever felt your body consuming a *bullet*? Most importantly…" He leaned into the table. "Have you ever been an *animal*? No need to answer that. It's not a quiz."

Dean Mitchell, Riley thought, was no longer human. He *looked* human, but this was not anything close to the man she'd once seen around town and talked to semi-regularly. This thing that was sitting at the table with Sheriff Palmer was a monstrous, amplified amalgam of Dean Mitchell's flaws.

"I don't have any idea what you're talking about," Palmer said.

"No *shit*."

"What are you trying to do?"

"Be honest."

"All right. So you threaten your wife, but that's not related to you being there today. Tell me about the email."

"Just letting her know I stopped by."

Palmer rubbed the bridge of his nose. "Elmer Kopps?"

"The night before the full moon is a *partial* transformation. It's your body preparing for what's to come. I woke up that next morning naked and piecing together memories. I needed clothes, so I killed him. It occurred to me after I did it that I'd done it."

"Savannah Golding?"

"She died right in front of me. I didn't kill her."

"Marion Golding?"

"Her either."

"What about her body?"

"I could smell her. Very well. So I found her and took her to where she wanted to go."

"Who killed her?"

"My opinion? Her daddy killed her. He ate the poisonous fruit of a poisonous family. He killed her, and after it was all over, he made his own exit. Don't expect the same from me."

"You've lost your mind."

"Thanks for the talk, Sheriff," the monster said.

30

LATE THAT AFTERNOON, KATELYN MET Robert and Riley at The Painted Lady. She was on her way to Harrison to see her husband, but Riley wanted to talk first.

They drank iced tea and nibbled at an order of chips and salsa. Riley requested that Katelyn tell them about her trip, but Katelyn shook her head.

"You first," she said. "You wanted to tell me something about the Evenware House."

"It's something, all right," Robert said.

Riley handed Katelyn her phone, which displayed a picture of what looked like a piece of red flannel lying in dirt.

Riley explained that they'd found it while digging beneath the Evenware House.

"We quit digging when we found it," Riley said. "It just about has to be Jonathan, but I don't want to know.

Right before we found it, *somebody* in the house said, 'You'll be the first to go, you bitch.' But we were alone."

Robert said: "There's some sort of plant growing out of his grave, right up through the floor."

Katelyn's shock must've shown on her face.

"What?" Riley said.

Katelyn said nothing. Simply retrieved the John Evenware letter from her purse and extended it to them.

Robert took it, unfolded it, and placed both pages near the center of the table.

For the next five minutes, both of her friends read quietly. As they read, Katelyn brought up a photo of Thomas Evenware's grave.

At last, they looked up.

Riley said: "Jonathon had it. Golding got it. And he passed it to your husband."

"What about the plants?" Robert nodded down at Katelyn's phone.

"'The poisonous fruit of a poisonous family,'" Riley said.

31

KATELYN SAT ALONE IN A little room not much bigger than a closet. There was another chair in the room, that was it. Behind her was the heavy door that would soon open and reveal her husband. She'd been in here less than a minute, and she already regretted it. She still had not rested. Last night in the Little Rock hotel room did not count. She just needed to go home.

The door opened and Dean Mitchell stepped in. He was thin, barely recognizable, dressed in white and orange jail garb, shackled and cuffed.

He neither smiled nor frowned as he sat down in the chair across from her.

The deputy in the doorway pulled the door shut.

There was a window in the wall to her left through which the deputies out in the corridor could watch them. But they were still alone, and Katelyn still regretted this. All of it.

Dean Mitchell kept his gaze on her. He said: "These county jails are such shit. It wasn't all that long ago I was in this room, wearing a suit, feeling so important as I cooled the jets of a lowlife druggy. Things change. Your perspectives change, too, if you're wise. I *knew* it was all nothing, yet I convinced myself that I was a critical cog in the gears of the greatest justice system in the world. The things we wish to believe."

She felt herself wanting to cry. The sight of him. Hearing his voice.

"Do you still love me?" she said.

"Do *you* love me?"

"I always did."

"Let me tell you something, Katelyn: You hurt me, minimized me, and accused me. These things were seldom done directly. I've never actually known you to be anything but kind. But I never was a fool, and I am sharper now than ever."

The threat—if that's what it was—hung visibly between them for a second.

Until what she'd just heard actually hit her, and she stood and knocked on the glass.

32

PALMER HATED HIMSELF FOR KNOWING the moon would be a "waning crescent" on this Wednesday night. He'd looked it up earlier today, because—and he hated admitting this—he was letting this ordeal get to him.

Okay, fine, you're curious. But surely none of that stuff is taking root in your head. Surely.

He was watching Dean Mitchell now. The man was sitting at a table playing rummy with another inmate. A very damaged man, but a *human being* nonetheless, not any sort of animal or mythical beast. He was a lawyer! Lawyers—generally—were brash, intoxicated, wretched people; toss in an unhappy marriage and an infected lump, and what will you get? Something like Dean Mitchell, sure thing.

A doctor who'd been looking at Dean Mitchell's neck while he played rummy came over and took a seat by Palmer, in a plastic chair along the far wall, as far away from the lawyer as the room allowed.

"Well?" Palmer said.

"It doesn't appear infected. If it was, it's not anymore. He wouldn't let me touch it, said it was getting better. I don't believe that, but that's what he said."

"Anything more? Are lumps the size of shooter marbles on a fella's neck normal?"

"Do you have one, Sheriff?"

"I'm asking for a local jackass."

"Lumps like that could be the result of an infection. It looks like a lymph node. If it's been there a long time, and especially if it's growing, it could be cancer. We'd need tests to know for sure. He's obviously not interested."

"I see."

"I would encourage your local jackass to get it checked out."

"I'll talk to him."

The doctor patted his shoulder and walked away. A deputy let him out of the room.

This was the *first* of two doctors Dean Mitchell would see, Palmer thought, recalling the previous day's spectacle during Mitchell's arraignment:

How do you plead?

As a man, Judge, I am not guilty. Later on, I'd give you a different answer, because the inhuman part of me is.

What are you doing, Mr. Mitchell? Don't we go back a good ways? Don't you think I know you?

You thought so, Judge.

Absurd, of course. Totally insane. But the *look* on Mitchell's face, that calm and disturbed arrogance in his eyes and across his lips—Palmer thought *that's* what really drove the judge to order a psychiatric evaluation.

185

And *that* doctor would be here tomorrow.

RILEY PULLED INTO THE HOME Depot in Harrison and parked at the back of the lot. She took a drink of the Sonic Coke she'd just bought and went to the Kyler Custom Weaponry site on her phone. She perused their inventory again, but did not click anything. She had questions to ask, and so she called the number at the bottom of the page.

A polite gentleman answered on the third ring, stating his name was Kyler, of Kyler Custom Weaponry, and how could he be of assistance?

Riley informed him she was thinking about making an order, but she had some questions.

"Sure thing," Kyler said. "I *am* this operation, so I can answer pretty much anything you ask."

"Do you deal with shotgun ammo?"

"I *can*. Filling shotgun shells isn't difficult."

"Can you fill a three-inch .410 cartridge with silver?"

"Sure. Honestly, ma'am, that's something you could do, or—"

"I imagine you're right, sir, but I wouldn't know where to begin, and I'm ordering something else anyway."

"Good, okay. Go on."

"Your silver nine-millimeter bullets. Nickel cased. Do they fire?"

"Yes, *but*. These bullets are meant as novelty items. I've put them in guns and fired them, others have as well. They're real bullets. They *are* more likely to jam, or that's what it seems like. I'd say that's true for any silver bullet you could find."

"Can I order over the phone?"

"Sure thing."

"Two nine-millimeter bullets, silver. Four .410 cartridges filled with silver buckshot. And can I get these shipped to Ellingwood, Arkansas within a week?"

"You know, I shipped some to Arkansas not all that long ago, .32s, to a joker who said his wife or daughter might need to kill a werewolf. What do you all have going on down there in Arkansas?"

SHE WENT INTO THE HOME Depot and went straight back to the outdoor lawn and gardening department, which was readying itself for the imminent spring season.

She had nobody in particular she was looking for.

She found an elderly employee unloading a crate of weed killer and asked him how much he knew about plants.

He stopped what he was doing and wiped his hands on his pants and said, "Well, I know some. But my wife knows a lot more than I do. You'll find her right over there at the cash register."

The woman running the machine was probably close to seventy. She was currently taking money from a young man who was buying a garden hose. Riley hung back, waiting, and approached the woman—*Margie*, her nametag said—when she was done.

"I was told you know about plants," Riley said.

Margie playfully rolled her eyes. "You've been talking to Mel, I bet. I know a little bit, or I like to think I do."

"Will you help me identify something?"

"I'll try."

Riley removed her phone and showed Margie a picture of the plant in the Evenware House.

The old woman leaned in, squinted, and adjusted her glasses. She studied the image for a long moment and finally shook her head.

"I just can't tell," she said, "though the flowers are pretty. Let's see what Mel knows. Mel!"

He'd been approaching anyway, as it turned out, and hurried his pace after Margie called his name. Margie handed him Riley's phone and asked him if he knew what this was.

Mel retrieved a pair of glasses from his shirt pocket, put them on, and studied the picture.

Then he looked up at Riley and said, "Can you look stuff up on this thing?"

She said she could.

"Try 'belladonna' or 'nightshade.'"

"Deadly nightshade?" Margie said. "Really?"

Mel shrugged. "It's not common, but you might find it around here. Not that big of a deal, unless you've been eating on it."

Riley typed the terms BELLADONNA DEADLY NIGHTSHADE into Google and compared the images the search produced to the one from the Evenware House. The leaves were potentially the same, but the bell-like purple flowers gave it away.

"It'll grow berries, too," Mel said. "Don't eat'em. A few of those and monsters'll be coming straight up out of the floor."

THERE WAS NO WINDOW IN his cell, but Dean Mitchell still saw the thick blackness of a dark February night and the millions of stars and thin sliver of moon that it contained. The shadows were either faint or nonexistent. The trees in the forest were as dark as the spaces between them. The night smelled like cold exhaust. Yes, he smelled it. Felt it, too. Because part of him was still out there. It was newfound knowledge and perspective.

He could smell the starry night.

But why was he in here? Because he was still—in many ways—human. Human enough to thus find himself sick and exhausted (particularly the former; he'd felt physically ill since long before the full moon). Human enough to sit down on the toilet and lose consciousness while engaging in a particularly stressful activity.

He smiled. It was all okay. This would all be fine.

He tasted a starry night.

He wished he could throw it up.

This will pass, he told himself, curled up on the bed, eyes open, closed, open again. *It always passes if you let it.*

Katelyn.

Her again.

Because the clearest path to becoming a monster is to hurt the ones you love.

You know you've arrived when you enjoy it.

189

33

THE NEXT MORNING, HE AWOKE to burning eyes and a
dull throb in the back of his skull. The lump on his neck
was tender again; merely applying his fingertips to it felt
like he was scraping it with sandpaper. Yet, he smiled.
And he was still smiling when he sat down at the folding
table across from a sharp-featured woman with fiery
hair who called herself *Doctor* Amanda Smelter. The all-
business type, Dean Mitchell immediately labeled her.

After she introduced herself, she asked his name.

He told her.

"And you're a lawyer?" she said.

"I was."

"Do you know why you're here?"

"In this room, or in this facility, generally?"

"Both."

"I'm in this room so I can talk to you, because my
old friend the judge thinks I might be *unfit*. I'm in this
facility because I killed Elmer Kopps. I pled not guilty,

and it's true, even though I did it. I would say I look forward to trial, but I doubt there will be one."

"Why?"

"Upcoming events."

"Like?"

"Hard to say."

"How old are you?"

"Forty-four."

"Married?"

"To Katelyn."

"Why did you kill Mr. Kopps?"

"I needed his clothes."

He thought Smelter might at least raise an eyebrow. But she acted as though she'd heard nothing at all.

"Tell me about your childhood, Mr. Mitchell."

KATELYN STOOD IN HER DRIVEWAY watching two Home Depot deliverymen carry her new front door into the garage and lean it against the wall. Robert had insisted there was no need for her to pay for installation when he'd love to do it himself. Just give his currently swollen joints a few days to go down; that's all he asked.

So the boys from Harrison left the door in the garage, thanked her for her business, and drove away.

Less than a minute later, as Katelyn was stepping inside, a silver Audi SUV pulled into the driveway. The engine shut off and a thirty-something, professionally dressed woman climbed out, adjusted her blouse and sunglasses, and started up the driveway.

Katelyn remained on the doorstep in the garage.

191

"I'm Dr. Amanda Smelter," the woman said upon reaching her. "I've been talking to your husband and hoped I could talk to you. Do you mind?"

"No. Come in. I'm sorry for how the house looks. I wasn't expecting anybody."

Katelyn showed her to the living room, and the doctor went straight to the boarded over door. She placed her hand on the plywood.

"Storm?" Smelter said.

"Husband."

They settled on either end of the couch.

"Does your husband believe he's a werewolf?" Smelter said.

"I don't know what he believes."

"Just give me your opinion."

"Yes. I think he believes that."

"Have you talked to him recently?"

"The day they arrested him. At the jail."

"How'd that go?"

"Depressing. I was scared."

"Did he know who you were?"

"Yes."

"Was he apologetic?"

"No. He blames me. For everything."

Smelter paused and rubbed the tops of her legs. "Just so you know, I am supposed to make a determination as to whether or not your husband is fit to proceed in his case. This is not a medical issue. Anything you tell me will help. I just have to figure out if your husband is aware of who he is and what's going on in his life. *Why* he's in the situation he's in."

"He knows what's going on," Katelyn said. "He's calculated. He's sane."

"Yet he thinks he's a werewolf."

Katelyn was tempted, so incredibly tempted, to tell—show—this woman everything. But Smelter was a doctor, a professional, and her demeanor indicated that no amount of deer camera images or personal horror stories would convince her that at least some, if not all, of what Dean had told her was true.

Nevertheless, Katelyn proceeded. Just a bit further.

"Maybe he is," she said. "In a way."

The look Smelter gave her was not one of *total* disbelief. There was patience in it. Curiosity.

"What do you mean?"

Katelyn nodded at the plywood over the doctor's left shoulder. "He knocked the door in, one try, no sledge hammer. Nothing. I don't know how that's possible. So I guess I can't tell you what I mean."

AMANDA SMELTER PULLED AROUND THE corner, put the Audi in park, and retrieved a spiral notebook and pen from the passenger seat. She clicked the pen and wrote, word after word, line after line—some of it direct quotes, some of it paraphrases—everything she could recall from the conversation she'd just had. She felt that both Dean Mitchell and his wife were prime case study material. Put them in books and let the kids tear them to pieces.

She was afraid she needed to see him again.

It was the cut, she decided, setting the notebook and pen down and opening her right hand to look at it.

193

Nothing much. Just a faint, half-inch red line near the center of her palm.

But there was no doubt: In saying goodbye to her, Dean Mitchell had assaulted her. Held out his cuffed hands, extended the right one as much as he could, and when she made the mind-numbing decision to actually *accept* his handshake, he casually (and not all that painfully) embedded one of his fingernails into her flesh. Minimal bloodshed.

No big deal, she told herself.

He probably didn't even mean to. Just one of those things.

But that was silly, and she knew it.

Katelyn had called him *calculated* and *sane*.

Smelter agreed with her. And somehow, though it was impossible, she thought he must be *honest* too.

34

THE ELDERLY GENTLEMAN WHO LIVED around the corner from Riley was a retired roofer who'd developed, over the past twenty or so years, a reputation for being a quality gunsmith. He'd done some cleaning and minor repairs for Riley in the past, but this was the first time he'd seen her grandfather's single-shot .410. She'd shot it only once, as a little girl, and knew almost nothing about the gun.

Certainly, she had no idea if the relic was still functional or not.

The gunsmith's name was Carr, and she'd brought him the gun at seven 'o clock this morning. It was now ten till noon on Friday, March 3.

Waxing crescent tonight.

They stood in Carr's shop building, looking down at the gun on his workbench. It was broken open, a shell in the chamber.

"Iver Johnson Champion, .410," Carr said. "Based on the serial number and the fact that it'll shoot a three-inch cartridge, I'd date it back to the forties. Cleaned it, that's all I did. It'll fire. Good gun. Not worth much—you might get a hundred for it. But it's a good gun."

Riley picked it up, snapped it shut. "Can I?"

"Nothing but woods out there. Go for it."

She took the gun behind the shed, aimed into the trees, pulled back the hammer, and squeezed the trigger. The kick was satisfying but, as expected, minimal.

"What do you think?" Carr said from behind her.

"I think I'll keep it," she said.

SHE SPENT OVER AN HOUR that afternoon helping Robert and Katelyn install Katelyn's new front door. When the chore was done, they settled into lawn chairs in Katelyn's back yard. Riley had something she wanted to discuss, and she was both excited and terrified to talk about it.

"After days of digging—*deep* digging—I found this, this morning, while a neighbor was working on one of my guns. I started out blindly trying to find the book Katelyn's picture came from. It didn't go well, obviously. But a couple of days ago I found out the plants on Thomas and Jonathon's graves are *Atropa belladonna*—deadly nightshade. It's not common around here. And it's very poisonous. So, I woke up early this morning and fed a convoluted search into Google Books. I think I searched 'Evenware Belladonna Idalia' plus the page and figure numbers that are on the page with the picture. I expected nothing, but I found it. It's all there. It's called *Folklore of the Full Moon*, published in London in 1934 by an author who..." She looked at a piece of paper in her hand and continued: "...'has spent time, for the purposes of this book, on four continents and who wishes to remain anonymous.' The book is a collection of personal accounts, folklore, beliefs, traditions, and it's all about demons and mythical creatures. I searched it for all our key terms. The author specifically recounts Thomas Evenware's death in a chapter about the history of silver being used to kill monsters. That's where the illustration is. According to the book, yes, the locals in Idalia believed he was a werewolf, and they shot him in the street with a silver bullet. Supposedly. And then there is this...."

She handed Robert a printout from the book.

Katelyn leaned in as Robert unfolded it:

Many associate lycanthropic activity and its origins with the full moon. The two most common sources of lycanthropic infection I encountered in my research were the drinking of rainwater from the print of a wolf during a full moon and the ingestion of certain poisonous herbs that grow or change in certain fashions during the full moon. Concerning the latter, I heard mentioned in several rural areas a direct correlation between the deadly nightshade and lycanthropic activity; specifically, a significant number of rustic folk believe a variant of the Atropa belladonna grows from buried remains of werewolves, and during nights of the full moon, its berries swell with the blood of the beast. All who ingest these berries will be infected with lycanthropy.

Perhaps the simplest and most direct way to contract lycanthropy is to be scratched or bitten by a werewolf, though some claim full infection depends upon the severity of the scratch or bite. Lycanthropy can be contracted by any means that allows the

197

infection access to one's blood, through ingestion or open wound. Put simply, lycanthropy is a contagion....

They did not speak, and the silence persisted for an indefinite period of time.

Riley excused herself, walked around to her Jeep, and returned with a cigar box. She opened it and distributed its contents: four shotgun shells. Two for Katelyn, two for Robert.

Robert held one of the shells up in front of his face. ".410."

"That's right." Riley sat back down. "Filled with silver. Crazy? Yes. If this all turns out to be lunacy, it can be our secret. Me, I've seen enough. I have two rounds for my gun. The shotgun's probably the best choice. And the .410's easy to fire. I wanted you two to have them."

"I don't believe I have a .410, Riley," Robert said.

Riley said: "I have one. It's old, but it's been cleaned, gone over, and fired."

Robert stuffed the shells in his pocket. "You don't have to convince me. I've already shot it once."

RILEY LEFT KATELYN'S HOUSE LATE that afternoon and drove a few passes through town. Next, she stopped at The Painted Lady and made herself a ham and cheese sandwich and sat in her Jeep alone, eating and listening to old country music at a very low volume. She turned the radio off when Ronnie Milsap started into "Stranger In My House."

She was not going home, she decided. Not yet. She could not. These things in her mind, realities that no part of her could believe, she *did* believe, and if she thought about that too long, she started losing it. So what good was home? It had a bed for when she got too exhausted to blink. That was it.

Too exhausted to blink. That's what it took for her to sleep nowadays, and she was not there.

And so, after her sandwich, she drove out of town to the End Zone, where the same old crowd was gathered at the bar, some of them watching the Cardinals on the TV above the mirror. They were used to seeing Constable Riley Saunders around; none of them thought anything of her being law enforcement. She was just a local woman who was only interested in having a drink and being left alone.

Tonight was the same. She went in, found an isolated seat at the bar, and told the bartender she wanted a gin and tonic.

She eased into the drink and told herself it'd be the only one.

The booze slowed her heart rate and calmed her, though it still did not allow her to accept loading silver bullets into a gun and shooting at a movie monster. Perhaps she was *close* to that point, however, because she'd seen what she'd seen and knew what she knew.

Such were her thoughts when the End Zone's front door opened and a man came in saying that something was burning; it was out in the woods on the other side of town, and "you can see the glow and smoke from here."

Riley pushed away the remnants of her drink and crossed the room to the door.

35

AFTER ROBERT AND RILEY LEFT, at 4:30 that afternoon, Katelyn found herself standing in an empty living room looking at her new front door with her shotgun propped next to it. Right next to the gun, on the little sewing table meant for keys and pocket change, were the silver-packed shells. A single tear trickled down her left cheek as she pondered whether or not she should scream, cry, or laugh. All were fine choices. Scream for the relief. Cry for what's gone. And *laugh* at the total fucking lunacy of it all.

Ultimately, she did none of the above. She took a deep breath and lay down on the couch. She tried to doze, and perhaps she did, but her eyes kept returning to the gun and the shells until she could not tolerate them anymore, at which time she got up and hid them under the couch. She then went into the kitchen and was searching for a bottle of something stout when she heard a knock on the door.

She paused. Returned to the living room. Just as the knocking came again.

It was neither Robert nor Riley. Neither of them would come to the front door, for one. And if they did, their knocks would probably contain more urgency. Palmer? Maybe. The doctor? Smelter? Again, maybe.

It *couldn't* be her husband, could it? He was in jail.

"Who is it?" she said.

Nothing. Except another knock.

Katelyn muttered a curse and dug the shotgun out from under the couch. She checked and saw that there was a standard buckshot shell in place. Not that she *needed* the gun, surely. This was overkill and paranoia, but so be it. She had her reasons.

She turned the deadbolt, gently opened the door… and nobody was there.

Don't play games with me, she thought, nudging the door open wider and stepping into the threshold—just to be knocked back into her living room as the shotgun was ripped from her hands.

Her butt and elbows hit the floor hard and she saw the man who entered her home with perfect, high definition clarity.

He's familiar, she thought. *He's…*

She'd seen this face before.

He was the stranger from the gas station in Maryland. Also known as Lewis Evenware. She'd seen him around town for years. She'd never talked to him, not once. And she hadn't put the name to the face when she'd first seen him in Maryland; she'd been preoccupied with finding the church and Thomas Evenware's grave.

201

But why this?

He stepped inside, tapped the door shut with the back of his left foot, and propped her shotgun against the wall by the door.

"I'm not here to hurt you." He stepped over her and sat down on the couch. "Not necessarily."

Katelyn dared sit up. The shaggy-haired skeleton on the couch leaned forward with his elbows on his knees, and there was now a huge revolver in his left hand. It was not aimed at her. It was not aimed at anything.

Maybe he hadn't come here to do anything rash.

But that didn't mean he wouldn't.

So she did not stand. She simply pulled her knees up to her chest and wrapped her arms around her legs. Look comfortable, she told herself. Look calm. Because this man was obviously neither.

"I saw you in Idalia," he said.

"I remember."

"I saw you see me. You were researching my family."

"Yes."

"I saw your car outside Paula's." He inhaled deeply, slightly shifted the revolver in her direction, exhaled. "I gave Constable Saunders my mama's message, to help. I couldn't remember anything. But I wanted to help. I am not a bad person. But do you know what happened when *I* tried to investigate? My own family—Paula— told me to get out! Did you tell her something about me?"

"Lewis—"

"Don't say my name."

"I did not tell her *anything* about you."

Lewis pressed a thumb into the bridge of his nose. "The night Mama died, I had a nightmare. I was burying my dad. But why? And why was your husband at my old house? Why was Mama having Golding tear it down? Why? I wanted to know.

"In Idalia, I went in that little church. I saw Thomas in there praying. He looked up at me, and he was dead, and he said, 'Even God won't save us.' And I believe him. So no, it doesn't matter. All I can do is try to rid the world of *us*. That's why I did what I did." Now he directed a finger at her. "Your husband has it now. So kill him." He picked up the revolver. "You have to kill him."

SHE SAT FOR A MOMENT in a haze, her stomach still aching where he'd applied his foot, and in the haze, she saw his face and heard his words. *That's why I did what I did.…* She sat in this haze for she didn't know how long, until it hit her, and she got up and locked the door and dialed Paula Evenware's number and paced the house, listening to the phone ring, hoping the old woman would answer. But she didn't answer.

She sat down on the couch and closed her eyes and almost cried herself to sleep, because she was suddenly tired—incredibly tired. She'd reached a point at which her body simply refused to do anymore. Just let it doze. She did. She…

Another knock on the door.

She looked up, mortified, knowing it was about to happen to her, too. Of course it was.

203

But when she opened the door, Riley was there. Just Riley.

"Are you okay?" Riley immediately said.

"What time is it?"

"Almost six thirty. Are you okay?"

Almost six thirty?

"Katelyn?" Riley said.

"It was Lewis Even—" She stopped when she heard sirens. "What's that about?"

"The Evenware House is burning. That's why I'm here. You said Lewis was here? What happened? "

But Katelyn did not explain. Not yet. She was suddenly awake and ready to go.

SHE TALKED AS RILEY DROVE. She had no problems recalling the details of Lewis's visit.

"I know he killed Paula," she concluded. "He knows something's wrong with his family. He doesn't totally understand, I don't think, but he's dangerous."

By the time Riley pulled up next to a volunteer fireman's Silverado in front of the Evenware House, the entire structure was an inferno, and the firemen were simply on a mission to save the forest.

The two women got out to watch. They stood back against the front of Riley's Jeep, and at some point, Sheriff Palmer joined them.

"No secret who it was." He pointed toward the top of the flames. "Right up there."

Katelyn saw him immediately. And she suspected *he* saw her.

The human figure had surely not been in the upstairs window the entire time, not standing there like the flames were nothing at all... waiting to be consumed, waiting for the floor to give way beneath him. Waiting. Surely not.

"He's been going back and forth from the window for a few minutes now," Palmer said. "You can tell it's that crazy ass Evenware kid. Frankly, he's done us all a favor."

A few minutes later, a substantial portion of the roof collapsed, followed by most of the second story.

36

DOCTOR AMANDA SMELTER FELL OUT of touch with reality. She'd felt fine the Thursday she met with Dean Mitchell (the Wolf Man, as she'd come to think of him). Heck, she'd been fine the day after that, too, and maybe the next day.... But by the next Friday, the wound the Wolf Man had dug into her palm was red and swollen and so incredibly tender that her hand was nearly unusable. She coated it in antibiotic ointment and dressed it in a thick bandage.

This wasn't her first time to be injured by a prisoner or patient. She'd spent the first six years of her psychiatric career at a small office in Maumelle, where she'd worked with a much older doctor named Evans. The old man already had a foot out the door and thus handed Smelter more work than she could possibly handle. This work included evaluating an alleged murderer suffering from schizoaffective disorder, who, in an attempt to illustrate his "anguish" to her, twisted her left arm behind her back and bit into the side of her neck like a vampire. There was also the rapist who'd head butted her and the patient named Marty who'd attempted to lick her and poked his nose into her right eye.

The nature of the business. All things considered, she'd done pretty well.

But Dean Mitchell was her first Wolf Man. He'd left his mark, too, and she wasn't yet done with her report.

Because she had no idea what to say about him.

The wound seemed to *somewhat* heal over that first weekend in March. On Sunday night, she undressed it, let it breathe for a few hours, then redressed it in a smaller bandage.

Monday morning, March 6, she went to her office to send emails and get the day's phone calls over with. Her office was in downtown Harrison, which was twenty miles from her home in a beautifully secluded wide spot in a county road called Deer Creek. She'd never minded the drive; being on the road was part of her career, since the "drive by" competence check was one of her specialties. And sometimes, the commute to and from work was what kept her sane. It was a time for music, thinking, planning, decompressing.

But on this Monday morning, she hated it.

By the time she got to work, all she could do was sit quietly and try to will and pray her sick stomach into settling.

It was the wound in her palm. She knew it, but she didn't understand it.

She peeled the bandage back and saw that the area was worse than it had been last night. Much of the tender, red puffiness was back, and the cut, which had (she thought) closed, was open again: GIVE ME YOUR GERMS, YOUR DIRT, YOUR INFECTED MASSES, it said… as it oozed and throbbed.

She went to the restroom and washed the wound with soap and water. She found a tube of Neosporin and a box of adhesive bandages in the cabinet above the toilet, and she redressed the thing all over again. She then leaned into the counter and performed the ancient ritual of looking straight into her reflection's eyes and telling herself to *get a grip.*

She was a professional. It was Monday morning. There was much to do. Yes, she had to get a grip.

This mindset got her through the day. She did, for a few extended periods, manage to forget the infection and get work done. But when she got home that night, she was convinced her entire arm hurt. *No big deal,* she told herself when she tried to relax. *You're not at work anymore. You're not distracted. Pains surface when there are no distractions.*

Tuesday was much the same—early morning breakdown followed by a few hours of productivity, fueled by her desire to forget about that which was driving her crazy. But Wednesday was bad. On Wednesday, she awoke at four a.m. to discover her hand was bleeding… badly. Furthermore, she was feverish, and if she recalled correctly, her sleep the last few hours had been restless and filled with bizarre dreams about demons.

She cleaned and re-bandaged the wound, but the blood would be impossible to get out of the sheets.

Her head was a mess. Her stomach, too. She did not go to work. She made coffee and barely drank it, and thus began an entire day of fretting about whether or not she should show her hand to her old friend Doctor Bauer, the only doctor she'd visited in the last six years.

She didn't. *Not that day.*

But she took Thursday off and drove to Harrison that morning and showed Bauer her right palm. He looked at it for a few seconds and told her she should keep it clean and keep an eye on it, and he was *sure* it would go away. She pressed him. Told him she'd already done all that. It was getting worse; she was feverish; it was becoming a distraction… and it *hurt*. He took her more seriously after that. He wrote a prescription for an antibiotic and repeated his wisdom about keeping it clean.

She started her antibiotic that night and returned to work on Friday, not sure if she was feeling better or not. She'd wrapped the wound tightly and told herself to leave it that way all day. *Don't look at it, don't do anything with it; keep it covered, take the pills, see what happens.*

After lunch on Friday, she accepted that she had to do so something she simply did not want to do: deal with Dean Mitchell. The pain in her right arm that pulsed outward and upward from the wound in her palm was telling her things she did not want to hear. And during a pacing session within her office that afternoon, she asked herself: *You don't believe it… do you?*

209

Why would she think this? This was new. Alarming.

No. She collapsed into her desk chair. *No.* And any thoughts that suggested otherwise were bullshit thoughts. She was a practical, educated, well-read woman who'd seen this sort of irrationality before. Maybe she'd never *specifically* met a "Wolf Man," but the underlying causes were the same. And while she wanted to *help* people, she would *not*, herself, indulge such... bullshit! Not only was Dean Mitchell *not* a werewolf— he knew he wasn't! He'd simply reached a breaking point, and some underlying issue in his life had taken the form of a monster. Then, instead of resisting it, he'd fed it. She'd seen this before, many times.

But how deeply rooted was his *monster*? Was he actually starting to believe it?

The wound throbbed and burned. She thought of his eyes, and she thought of the plywood over Katelyn's door.

Do I believe him?

No! And she swore it, again and again.

But she *did* need to know if the "monster" had taken over. That was the issue she had to clarify.

If he truly believed he was a "Wolf Man," there was a good way to find out.

Her notes reminded her that the night *before* the February full moon had been an active night for the wolf man. And if he *were* absolutely insane, she'd be wise to avoid the night *of* the full moon. He'd already left a mark on her. No need to walk right into another.

It was Friday. Sunday was the full moon.

So, tomorrow.

She'd speak with him tomorrow night, hear what he had to say, see how *monstrous* the ninety-nine percent moon rendered him.

A bolt of pain shot out of her palm.

Why was she doing this?

She closed her eyes, shook her head, and called Sheriff Palmer.

"You know you believe me."

She picked her head up off the desk and made eye contact with the man sitting across from her. He'd dragged up one of the plastic chairs by the door, and he smelled of shit and pine needles. His eyes were round, inhuman, sometimes silver, sometimes green, depending on the subtle movements of his head.

Her desk and the papers on it were smeared with blood, and she assumed her face was, too, since that's where it had been up until a few seconds ago.

He said it again, *You know you believe me*, but she barely heard it.

His stink was too distracting.

"I don't believe you." She *thought* she said it. "How did you get in here?"

"I can go anywhere I want to go."

"I don't believe you."

"Yes you do." He pulled a tissue from a box on her desk and extended it to her. "You need to clean your hand. It's bloody."

She took the tissue.

"I didn't come here to scare you." Dean Mitchell smiled pleasantly and his teeth were long and sharp and

211

metallic. "I just want to remind you that you are mine. I'll see you tomorrow, Doctor."

37

SHERIFF PALMER TOLD HIMSELF REPEATEDLY that nothing was going on, and the rational part of him believed it. But there was no denying how strange it was that Amanda Smelter wished to talk to Dean Mitchell tonight. It was a Saturday! Whatever her thoughts about the man, crazy or not, Mr. Mitchell would still be in jail on Monday morning. That was, after all, the nature of it.

If you don't mind, Sheriff, I'd like to see him tomorrow night. I know it's a Saturday.

Sure thing, he'd said, *no problem.*

But he dreaded going to the jail tonight.

Why did Smelter want to see the lawyer again? The answer to *that* could be (and probably was) pretty easy: She didn't have a solid enough read on him to write her report. That, Palmer thought, was fine, understandable. The *timing* was the issue. Saturday night, the night before the full moon. Surely the doctor wasn't buying into Mitchell's horror movie act.

213

That evening, about an hour before Smelter was to arrive, he (reluctantly) got himself together and drove to the jail. Whatever happened, or didn't happen, he wanted to be around for it. There would be minimal drama tonight.

He found Mitchell sitting at a table in the common area playing cards with a kid who'd allegedly pulled a knife on a cop. Palmer told the kid to go play with himself for a minute, and he sat down across from the lawyer.

"Doctor Smelter is coming back here, tonight. She must think you're special."

"Have you told my wife?"

"I haven't told your wife anything. I'm just warning you."

"Warning me."

"Don't pull anything tonight."

"What could I possibly 'pull'? Tell me. I'd like to know your thoughts."

"I don't owe you my thoughts."

"Have you ever seen anybody batter or kill somebody who comes to visit them in jail? How exactly would that go down? I just want to know your thoughts."

Dean mindlessly shuffled the cards.

"I don't have any thoughts about you," Palmer said.

Dean Mitchell flicked him a card, face down, then took one for himself. "You first."

Palmer thought about sliding the card back across the table and telling the weirdo to go to hell, but he didn't, and he didn't like what occurred to him as he

214

flipped his card over to reveal the queen of spades. The queen of spades was his life. Right there on the table. Crazy, sure, but there it was. *That's my thought, jackass.*

Dean Mitchell turned over his card: nine of diamonds.

"Good for you, Sheriff. Tell Doctor Smelter I'm looking forward to it."

AMANDA SMELTER WAS IN A fog when she pulled up at the county jail; she felt like she was drunk while in the midst of a bad cold. She knew who and where she was, and on a superficial level, she knew why. Beyond that, the world was simply floating by. The fog was significantly worse now that she was at her destination.

She pulled into a parking spot near the jail's front entrance and a dull throb crept up her right arm. She felt the wound in her hand burning and stinging and oozing. Truly, she had to get this dealt with. This was very uncomfortable and concerning, and here she was at the county jail on a Saturday night, so she could talk to a man who believed himself a werewolf, and maybe *that* needed to be dealt with, too.

She grabbed her notebook and pen and reminded herself this was necessary. This was business.

Or maybe she was here for another reason entirely.

Was she looking forward to talking to him? *Do I believe him?*

Palmer had said the door would be unlocked, and it was.

She entered the building and checked her phone as she did so. Seven 'o clock. The moon would rise within half an hour.

Palmer was waiting for her at the check-in desk.

"Right back here," he said. "I'll take you to him."

She heard herself reply—*Thank you, yes,* or something—but she really was in a fog, and all she could think, as Palmer opened the heavy door, was: *What is wrong with me?* Answer: *This man I'm going to see.*

Sheriff Palmer led her through the first of the heavy doors, and they turned right into a bland, concrete corridor. Down twenty or so feet, then a left, through another heavy door... and here she was in a small room with the man who'd made her crazy.

He sat calmly at the folding table, cuffed hands in his lap, no expression at all on his face. His eyes locked on hers as she sat down across from him.

Behind her, Palmer said something, a faint whisper in the fog, and stepped out and pulled the door shut.

The fog seemed to lift a bit as she realized she was disgusted with herself for being here.

"This is going to be a good night," Dean Mitchell said.

"Did you intentionally hurt my hand?"

"Hard to say, since I don't remember hurting your hand."

Still no expression on his face, just the same old nothing that had been there since she stepped through the door, yet she was sure that he was different.

Physically different.

Craziness, too much imagination. She was too consumed by his stories.

216

No. It was true. He *was* different, and the moon would be cresting the horizon right about… now.

"I want to talk to you," she said, "about…"

She trailed off. There was no denying it: The man's face was different than it had been just twenty seconds ago. Nothing big, not yet. The bones above his eyes, for instance, appeared to have shifted subtly; they were now protruding, casting larger shadows down the expanse of his cheeks. The bridge of his nose had expanded, was *still* expanding. Visibly.

This had to stop. She wanted to say something, ask him what in the world was going on. But all she could do was look at him!

His smiling mouth was somehow emerging from his face and dragging his nostrils with it.

Dean Mitchell placed his cuffed hands on the table, though they should've been linked to the shackles on his ankles.

But the cuffs were broken and twisted and only a few links of the chain that had connected them to his feet remained.

When he saw that she'd noticed the cuffs, he winked.

And right there, right in front of her, she watched his ears grow sharper and taller.

"Come on, Amanda." His sounded as if he were struggling to breathe. "What did you want to talk abou—"

He choked on the last word and broke into a series of deep, reverberating coughs.

Patches of thick, ugly hairs, gray and brown, sprouted from his face and neck.

217

She was entranced, and so it did not occur to her that she had to *get out,* until the thing on the other side of the table hacked so deeply that blood spewed from its mouth and nose.

Several droplets splattered her, and she scooted away from the table and moved in what felt like slow motion toward the door. She heard it say something— *Thank you, Doctor Smelter*—except it didn't, because it could no longer talk—*I couldn't have done it without you.*

The door opened just as Smelter began to pound on it, and for a fleeting second, she thought she could escape and break its nose on the door face. But the thing grabbed her right shoulder and used her as a shield as it shoved its way out into the corridor.

Smelter immediately noted a deputy to her left and Sheriff Palmer to her right.

Just beyond Palmer was the heavy door that led to the exit.

The deputy had his gun drawn, but it was aimed at the floor, and the dumbstruck expression on his face suggested he would not soon be shooting anybody or anything.

The deputy spoke, his voice barely audible: "Mr. Mitchell?"

The thing, its right hand painfully clinching her shoulder, turned Smelter toward Palmer.

The sheriff was a dozen or so feet away, feet spread, gun clasped confidently in both hands.

"You've proven your point, Dean." Horrified awe was all over Palmer's face. "We all believe you now."

The creature raised its free arm and aimed a crooked, hairy finger toward the sheriff, then started toward him with Smelter still serving as a shield.

Smelter focused on the pointing arm. It was easier that way, to focus on this one thing; forget about the door, forget about the shocked awe on Palmer's face... just that one thing, its partially-transformed left arm. The sleeve of its garb ended at the elbow, and the limb beyond it was pale, streaked with blue veins, and dotted with random splotches of nasty hair. The finger way out there beyond it ended with a yellow, inch-long, slightly curled nail.

And now, the claw was just a few feet from the sheriff's gun.

The sheriff would not do anything that would risk her safety. Nor would the deputy behind her. But only God knew what the thing that held her would do—and what might happen as a consequence.

"Give it up." Sheriff Palmer's voice emerged weakly from behind the gun. He cleared his throat and continued with slightly more authority: "You've got no way out of here. Let her go. Give it up. Whatever's wrong with you, we'll deal with it, tell it to the judge. You know that."

The thing jabbed its outstretched finger toward the sheriff and emitted a dry gasp that might have contained an expletive.

And that was when Smelter caught the slight shift in the sheriff's eyes.

Smelter heard the *thunk* as something hit the back of the thing's head; the grip on her shoulder disappeared, and she lunged forward, hitting the wall to

219

Sheriff Palmer's right and spinning around just in time to see the creature take a swing at the deputy, who was bringing his baton around again. The creature's right hand struck the deputy's shoulder and sent him into the wall, and ultimately to the floor.

The monster turned back to Smelter and the sheriff.

In the seconds before it attacked, she made a conscious decision to take it all in. She had to. If she lived through this, she had to remember it: It was still more man than wolf. Its eyes and ears were totally animalistic, its nose and mouth partially so, definitely distorted out of typical human shape. Its fur coating was irregular and thin; in places (such as its face) it was nonexistent. But everything about the thing, including its noisy breathing and hunkered stance, was less than human.

If she weren't so captivated, she might be dead from the sheer horror of it.

It lunged at Sheriff Palmer.

He somehow remained calm, kept his feet planted, and fired a round at point blank range into its shoulder. The hit was solid, but it staggered the thing for less than a second. The monster attacked again, bringing its right hand around and delivering a solid blow to the side of the sheriff's head. Palmer stumbled, clearly dazed—and more gunfire erupted, two shots from the corridor's opposite end.

Smelter thought she screamed; it was hard to tell. The gunfire was so incredibly close and deafening.

"Watch it, goddamn it!" Palmer cried out.

But the deputy's shots had apparently made contact. The creature dropped to its knees and threw its head back and let loose a pained, weak, guttural noise that was unlike anything Smelter had ever heard. And then it lurched its head forward, gagged, and vomited a steady flow of lumpy, blood-laced, foul-smelling cream.

Nobody approached.

Smelter dared a light step backward.

Is this it?

Surely it was. It had been shot three times.

But it put a hand on the wall and climbed shakily to its feet.

No words. No gunfire. Just tense silence as it first limped, then walked, to the door that led to the exit.

It could not open it, of course. The door was metal. And locked. And the remains of Dean Mitchell certainly could not disengage it.

The monster grasped the door handle—which was built into the door, not merely attached to it—and attempted a futile tug. When the door did not open, it tried again, this time a bit harder. Still nothing.

Smelter pressed back against the wall, her eyes glued to this silent, puzzling sight.

The monster tugged the door handle again.

But the door did not consider moving.

Still, it persisted.

It was on the fourth attempt that Smelter—and everybody else, she assumed—heard something break.

Sheriff Palmer shook some stars out of his head and raised his gun.

"Forget it, Dean. Turn around."

The Dean Mitchell thing turned its head.

It was smiling, a few traces of vomit smeared on its lips, one hand still on the handle.

"Forget it," the sheriff said.

It pulled the handle again. There was a loud *snap* and *clank* as something broke, and it swung inward.

Sheriff Palmer's eyes widened. He almost dropped the gun.

The creature removed its hand from the handle and once again directed a dirty nail at the sheriff's face. With its other hand it reached into its breast pocket and removed a playing card. It dropped the card and the sheriff's head descended as it followed its course to the floor: the queen of spades.

Sheriff Palmer looked up.

"Stop, Dean," he said.

But the creature fled.

38

RILEY AND KATLELYN WERE IN Riley's Jeep, parked in a lumberyard's parking lot, right across the street from the jail. The Jeep was off. Neither woman had spoken much. They were waiting on they knew not what and were anxious for it to happen, if it were going to.

The moon, fat and orange, hung low and was visible through the trees on the edge of the lumberyard's property.

Riley watched the jail. Dark and quiet. And she wondered why she hadn't thought of coffee.

A silver Audi had pulled in about ten minutes ago.

Just now, Katelyn said, "That's the doctor's SUV."

"The psychiatrist?"

Katelyn nodded. "Smelter."

Several more minutes passed.

And then a series of muffled *pops*.

The women exchanged glances.

A minute or two later, the jail's front entrance burst open. A shadowy figure sprinted out into the darkness.

SHERIFF PALMER WAS OUT IN the lot by the time Riley and Katelyn were across the road and approaching the front of the building. He lit a cigarette and smoked in the light of the lot's single lamp.

"I don't believe a thing I just saw," he said.

Sirens from somewhere beyond the building.

Palmer tossed down his barely smoked cigarette and crushed it with his boot. "And I've already talked about it too long."

THE SHERIFF SHOULD HAVE ASKED what they'd seen, what it looked like, where it went—not that either of them could have said much.

But he'd been too shaken, and for Riley, that spoke volumes. Sheriff Palmer was a difficult man to shake.

They returned to the Jeep.

Before Riley started it, she asked Katelyn what she'd seen.

Katelyn pointed toward the northeast, toward the vast, rolling shadow between the jail and the moon that the locals called Potato Hill.

Riley agreed.

She pulled out of the lumberyard and started east, toward the hill and the silver moonlight.

39

ROBERT GOT THE CALL FROM Riley at a quarter after eight. It actually happened: Dean Mitchell was gone.

Robert was speechless for a moment. He was sitting on Katelyn's front steps with Riley's old single-shot loaded and propped against the rail behind him. *I'll hold the fort down here*, he'd said.

In a way, he'd cherished the idea of finishing the bastard off.

Now, he wasn't so sure. Could be he hadn't actually expected anything to happen.

"Was it him?" His phone was shaking against his ear. "Or the other thing?"

"We were across the street. It was dark. Are you still at Katelyn's?"

"Sitting right here. I can be here as long as I need to be."

He wasn't nearly as confident as he sounded.

Riley told him to be safe and be in touch, then ended the call.

Robert tried to imagine the scene in the jail. How, exactly, had it gone down? Who was hurt or dead? Anybody? The images his imagination conjured were mind numbing and were not conducive to remaining calm.

He wandered out into the yard and paced, following back and forth an invisible line from the sidewalk to the deer camera at the edge of the property.

Maybe we're wrong, he thought. *People need labels and names. We're so quick to apply them. Maybe this isn't what it looks like.*

But did it matter what they called it?

It was real, it was out there, and it hadn't died when it took a rifle shot to the head.

He stopped in the middle of the yard to reflect on this… and found himself looking due east, at the rising moon.

Nearly full, missing only the slightest sliver. Its low horizon orange was fading to yellow. Next it would settle to pale yellow as it arched across the middle of the sky.

A bellowing racket blew out of the night, and Robert dove for cover as a yellow Camaro bumped the curb and shot across Katelyn's yard.

It was gone as soon as it was there, and the street was quiet again—until a white pickup going a much more reasonable speed came around the corner, and for just a second, Robert thought it was going to pass by.

But the truck stopped in front of the house, and the passenger window came down.

226

Robert approached cautiously.

There were two men in the truck, both middle-aged, both white, and two rifles hung on a rack behind their heads.

Robert stood at the window, hands in his jacket pockets.

"This is the lawyer's house, ain't it?" the driver said.

"This is Katelyn and Dean Mitchell's house."

"Yeah, the lawyer. Who're you?"

"A friend. Who are you?"

"Concerned citizen. Son of a bitch didn't do a fuckin' thing for me a few months back but take my money. I'm looking forward to dragging his ass back to Palmer. Sorry motherfucker."

The driver eased his foot off the brake as he raised the window, and the truck rolled away.

Clearly, it was out. Probably the Internet. Nowadays, every miserable thing in existence either started there or took the shortest path to it. Robert hadn't much of a clue how social media or message boards or anything of the sort worked, but undoubtedly, some foolish deputy with a cell phone had posted *something*.

Robert returned to the porch and waited to hear from his friends.

AT THREE THIRTY IN THE morning, both Palmer and Riley addressed a small but enthusiastic group of "concerned citizens" that paused their search efforts in Riley's front lawn, all so they could *demand answers*.

"All you're doing is taking this community's only law enforcement officer—me—away from what I should be doing," Riley said. "Dean Mitchell could be in Ellingwood by now. And the time I'm spending here is time I'm not looking for him."

Palmer said through a bullhorn: "You folks need to go home and lock your doors. This man escaped and you need to assume he's dangerous. That's what you need to know, and it's all we've got for you, anyway. Quit standing on your constable's lawn distracting her from a job she's doing for free!"

And that's what they did. Supposedly. But the damage was done.

"SO NO," RILEY SAID TO Robert at six a.m., on Katelyn's front porch, "I didn't get any sleep last night, and no, we didn't find him."

"You need to get some sleep."

"I'll try for an hour or two. Then I'm starting over. We saw him run toward Potato Hill. That's where I'm going. Our search last night got cut short by those assholes in my yard. All because one of Palmer's guys sent his wife a text about the 'wolf man being loose."

"I'll stay here till she wakes up," Robert said, "and I'll be back this evening."

Riley patted his back. "God bless you, Robert."

40

BEFORE RILEY LEFT ELLINGWOOD, SHE went to Dean Mitchell's office. The front and back doors were locked, but she picked the lock on the back door easily with the lock pick set she kept in her Jeep. She'd only used the set once before—on her own front door—but the standard knob lock offered little resistance.

Once inside, she found his office unremarkable. The general disorder on his desk and partially filled coffee cup on his desk indicated that he'd been in here *fairly* recently, but when? And did it matter?

Several books had been removed from one of the shelves behind his desk. They were stacked haphazardly near the desk's left edge, except for one, which was broken open in the center. Riley used the tip of a single finger to raise the front just enough to read the title: *Torts: A Survey of Case Law, Second Edition.*

One of his law school texts, Riley figured, and she looked closely enough to see that the book was open to

229

the midst of a case titled *Katko v. Briney*, from the Iowa Supreme Court. Riley scanned a few lines, something about an intruder being shot with a spring gun, then moved away from the desk, taking a close look at everything and touching nothing. At the end of her search, she journeyed up the exterior steps along the building's back wall and found the door to his private little "apartment" closed but unlocked.

She stepped into a mostly empty room that contained only his chair. Maybe he'd been in here recently, maybe not.

Riley left it all as it was and set out again.

She drove south to Harrison and cut off the main road past the county jail onto Potato Hill Road. She and Katelyn had driven the road last night all the way to its intersection with US 65, and they hadn't found anything except a Camaro full of fools.

But things could be different in the daylight.

Potato Hill Road was paved for its first three miles, until it began the gradual ascent up its namesake bump.

Riley drove slowly, shifting her eyes constantly from one side of the road to the other.

Yes, she was well outside of her jurisdiction. Yes, this area was probably well covered already. No, she did not care about either of these facts.

She passed an empty patrol car shortly before the road turned to a stomach-jostling mix of dirt and massive rocks. She came to a near stop and craned her neck as she looked out the passenger window. Two deputies were out in a clearing beyond the patrol car. She wondered if they'd found anything... and decided she'd know soon enough.

She pressed on, keeping the Jeep at a steady crawl and putting it in four-wheel-drive as she crept up and around the southwestern slopes of Potato Hill. She stopped several times and sat and looked. Waiting for something to happen. Waiting to notice something. But always, nothing. Just a quiet, cool, sunny day.

Over an hour after turning onto Potato Hill Road, she reached US 65, the major north-south alleyway through the heart of the Ozarks. Beyond the highway, Potato Hill Road narrowed even more and continued on, generally northeast. Last night, she and Katelyn had taken a left on the highway and started back toward Ellingwood.

Now, after a patrol car passed by, she crossed 65 and continued.

The scenery opened up; the forest thinned and retreated from the road, leaving behind grass and boulders and fallen trees.

Eventually, she came to a creek crossing.

And there was no bridge.

Riley got out of the Jeep and approached the edge of the water.

She'd never been this far down Potato Hill Road, but she was sure this was Rinney Creek. Somewhere northeast of here, before it met the White River, this creek became a considerable force, nearly a small river itself. But here, there wasn't much to it. It wasn't even ten feet across, and it was very shallow. Her Jeep could cross it, no problem.

But had *Dean Mitchell* crossed it? If he'd come this way at all, had he forded the mighty Rinney Creek? Had he turned one way or the other and perhaps followed it?

If he'd followed it, one way would lead him toward Ellingwood; the other would take him, eventually, to the river.

He had no reason, she thought, to go to the river.

But the other two scenarios were possible.

She did not have to search long for clues. The remains of a footprint were in the mud on the opposite side of the creek. It was faint and not obviously Dean Mitchell's or anybody else's. But it *was* a footprint, and it was aimed away from the creek.

Riley crossed the water, using two large rocks as stepping-stones. A little further up the road, she found more tracks, these even fainter than the one by the creek, as the ground here was dry and hard.

She wondered if Palmer or any of his deputies had been out here. She assumed so and decided she'd wait a bit, see if she found something more substantial, before she contacted him.

But these new tracks confirmed that she'd leave the Jeep where it was. No need in destroying the trail.

Besides, Potato Hill Road—what there was left of it—did not go much further.

She'd checked the map on her phone multiple times and now checked it again; the faint gray line beyond US 65 ended less than a quarter of a mile beyond Rinney Creek.

She continued on the course, until, ten minutes later, she came to a curiosity.

To her left, a set of rugged tire tracks intersected with Potato Hill Road. They led generally north, first across a swath of grass and rock, and then into a patch of woods.

232

Riley checked her phone again.

Whatever this path was, it was not on the map.

But if it held out for maybe ten miles, it'd hit Highway 307, which led right to Ellingwood.

She found a toppled, rusted sign in the grass to the right of the road. It was in bad shape but still readable: CR 462.

She'd never heard of this road and suspected she wasn't alone.

This was an interesting curiosity. *If* he'd been here, which route would he take? Straight ahead, which soon turned to nothing, or...?

She stood silently and considered things.

The tire tracks appeared to parallel US 65 and Rinney Creek. But it was a different sort of route. For a renegade psychopath (the most optimistic term she could apply to Katelyn's husband), this "CR 462" came with a number of perks: It was (apparently) not shown on maps; it was a dry and disastrously rough "road" that would not allow for many visible footprints; and being in such rough shape, it would naturally present challenges for pursuers, whether on foot or in a vehicle.

Take it, she thought.

She decided to spare her feet and legs the torment of this road, which could feasibly go on for ten miles or more.

She had no choice but to go get her Jeep.

APPROXIMATELY FOUR MILES DOWN 462, she came to a scene that was eerily similar to what had been found at Elmer Kopps's property: a collapsing shack of a house

233

at the end of a dirt driveway, complete with a body in the lawn. The dome of the dead man's stomach soared like a bald mountaintop from the dirt and weeds of the lawn.

She left her Jeep on the side of the road and drew her gun as she approached the body.

The stench was ripe, tremendous, unmistakable.

The man was obviously dead and had been for sometime.

Various parts of the corpse, including his face and limbs, had been clawed and gnawed, destroyed, turned into a glossy, bloated, red-tinted landscape of decomposing gore.

Riley turned to the house.

She said Dean Mitchell's name, then regretted it.

Silence.

A cool breeze carried the squawk of a distant bird.

Riley approached the shack.

The front door was standing open, exposing the dirty bare plywood on the other side of the threshold.

God, the stench.

Riley stepped into the doorway.

To her right was a small, sad kitchen: a counter with a sink, a miniature refrigerator on the floor, a microwave on top of it. Scattered on the counter were jars of unknown substances, scattered electronics, clipped pieces of wire, a portion of what had once been a clock. Someone had been working on something, and Riley wasn't sure she liked what it was.

To her left, sprawled across the plywood, was a large, decomposing, and partially-eaten woman in a sea of her own blood and filth.

234

On the wall behind her, written in her fluids in letters two feet high, was the word
KATELYN.

41

"Their names were Darl Burrus and Pamela Skinner." Palmer paused to light a cigarette, and they continued down 462, the sheriff in one tire track, Riley in the other. "Jennings said they might've been dead for a month. At least a few weeks. The... chew marks are new. Like, last night new."

Palmer and Randall Jennings, the coroner, had arrived together; Palmer had left his Explorer at the creek and caught a ride in Jennings's 4x4 Tundra. It hadn't taken Palmer long to see and smell enough, and here they were, walking, wanting to be away, theoretically looking for more footprints. Not finding any.

"A few weeks," Riley said. "While Mitchell was off the grid."

But he came back last night... to eat?

She glanced down at her watch. Not yet noon. But she felt as though she'd been out here all day.

"I have a confession, Riley." Palmer stopped, smoked, gazed back at the truck and Jeep that were slipping further and further behind them. "I have to believe you. Elmer Kopps. Marion and Savannah Golding. These two. Pick any of those dead folks, and I've never seen anything like it. We've got all of them. And what I saw last night..." He shook his head. "I don't like to admit it or think about it. It was what it was."

They were walking again, into an eerie, rural silence that was almost as unsettling as the horror behind them.

"That thing," Palmer continued, "got shot and shot again, and it tore the door open and kept on going. How am I supposed to feel about that? I don't know. I'll say this, though. I know you're not crazy. I saw it, too. But I still can't believe this is some creature out of a Stephen King book. No ma'am. I still can't believe that."

They walked on.

The truck and the Jeep were no longer in sight.

"But I understand." He stopped again, tossed down his cigarette, stepped on it. "I'll have nightmares forever. I get it. And I'll be there tonight, with y'all, for the Mitchell woman, wherever you want or need me."

Riley took a moment, but she thanked him.

She wasn't ready to go back. So they went on.

WHILE RILEY AND PALMER TALKED, Katelyn remained in bed and dreamed about a song. She dreamed she was upstairs strumming her guitar, and a soothing chord progression unfolded. That familiar *I can work with this* confidence bloomed in her mind and hands. When the lyrics came, she knew she was dreaming, because lyrics *never* came like this. And they were terrible. Awful things, these lyrics, and she didn't have the best voice, anyway, just good enough, but that didn't matter; the best voice in the world couldn't make these words sound pleasant. *Do I love you enough to kill you? Do I love you enough for that?*

She dreamed she was playing her college girl Ibanez electric through the Line 6 amplifier, never mind that the Ibanez was missing a string and the Line 6 amp hadn't worked since W's first term. This was almost amusing. Almost. Until the amplifier, after the second chorus—*Do I love you enough to kill you? Do I love you enough for that?*—, emitted a high-pitched shriek that quickly transitioned into something almost organic; the last chord she'd strummed (C?) held on tight, but the amplifier transformed it into a howl. And the volume grew and grew and grew…

Until it opened her eyes.

EARLY EVENING. THEY WERE EATING a quiet meal around Katelyn's dinner table. Chicken strips and green beans. Riley had stopped at the diner on her way back from showering and changing clothes ("I feel like I have Darl Burrus all over me. I'll pick up supper.") Riley sat to Katelyn's left, Robert to her right. Katelyn thought the silence would eventually lead to conversation. But there was nothing left to talk about. They'd searched. The sheriff's department was searching. The Harrison police department. The state police. Palmer had come by the house this afternoon and asked to look things

238

over. He'd wandered the house and property, saying he was concerned. Concerned that they didn't know where Dean Mitchell was, concerned about some things he'd seen in Darl Burrus's shack this morning.

But if something *were* going to happen, it would be tonight.

Beliefs be damned, that was a fact.

At sunset, Robert took a liter of water, the .410, and his .30-06 out to the storage building in Katelyn's back yard.

He left the door partially open, sat down in a lawn chair, propped his feet on the back of the Mitchells' mower, and waited for moonrise.

PALMER KNOCKED ON THE FRONT door at six 'o clock.

Katelyn answered and found him on her porch, his hat in his hand. She invited him in, but he declined.

"I don't know what's going to happen. But I'm going to make myself invisible. I'll pull in at the church a few blocks back and be on foot. Any particular place you want me?"

Riley had stepped up beside Katelyn. When Katelyn didn't answer, Riley told him they trusted his judgment.

An hour later, Riley went out into the darkness.

Katelyn, now alone, went to the front window and looked out and saw that the eastern horizon was already faintly aglow.

Moonrise, and she was alone. She *wasn't*, of course, but her nerves didn't believe that.

She sat down on the couch. The Mossberg was on the coffee table in front of her.

Where was he now? Where would he come from?

Or will he come at all?

He called to her from upstairs. He said her name in a perfectly normal, human voice. He sounded calm, as if this were another time, back when everything was more or less okay.

Surely this isn't real.

But his voice came again: "Katelyn."

She rose from the couch and reached down and wrapped her hands around the gun.

"Just you, Katie. None of your friends. You and me."

The sane thing, the smart thing, would be to run. Straight through the front door, into her car, cross the county line, the state line, cross every line she could until she was at the most random point imaginable, an eternity away. Let her maniacal husband be somebody else's problem.

But she couldn't do that. She'd come too far down this proverbial road. The man, or monster, upstairs was her husband; he was her problem. And maybe, in some bizarre way, she was partially responsible for all of this. Had her selfish tendencies (*Am I selfish?*) contributed to their marriage's decay? Had *she* helped turn him into a more wretched creature than the man the Good Lord originally made? Silly, she thought, but not really.

She had to go upstairs.

She clinched the shotgun, suddenly aware of what it was for.

Halfway up the stairs, the melancholy resonance of a strummed A-minor chord wafted through the attic door. This made sense. Her husband knew four or five of the open chords, A-minor being one of them.

Before entering the room, she sent a text to Robert, simply because she saw his name first: *Upstairs.*

Then she tucked her phone away, took a deep breath, readied the shotgun, and somehow found the strength to step through the door.

She found him sitting on the Line 6, her go-to Breedlove resting on his right knee, the fingers of his left hand still fretting the chord he'd strummed. He was human—frail, gray, expressionless. He rested his arms atop the guitar and again said her name.

Katelyn almost relaxed. Almost let the shotgun fall to her side. Almost.

"How did you get in?" she asked.

The octagon window at the end of the room was still screwed shut.

"Back door," he said.

"The back door is locked."

He plucked a few strings. "It's over, Katie. It was over before this happened. Maybe, had all this *not* happened, we would've toughed it out for another year. But let's be honest, we are the epitome of the love-hate dichotomy. I love you dearly, yet I loathe the deepest parts of you. Do you see?"

Her eyes, goddamn it, were welling.

He leaned over the guitar as if he were truly trying to persuade her: "Mutual existence is no longer an option. I'm hungry, Katie, and one of us won't leave this room."

241

He leaned back. Point proven. The look on his face was *so* arrogantly confident. *So* Dean Mitchell.

The guitar, she noticed, was shaking.

FROM THE EAST END OF the house, directly below the octagon window, Riley watched the moon break over the horizon. Just seeing the light caused her stomach and chest to hurt. And it wasn't just nerves, either. She felt something else.

And she knew to trust herself.

Something was wrong.

She retrieved her phone from the cargo pocket of her pants and sent Robert a text: *Going inside.*

ROBERT RECEIVED TWO TEXT MESSAGES within a few seconds of each other.

He debated for only a few seconds whether he should follow Riley into the house. Would he be better served out here?

No. She could not go in there alone.

He slung the deer rifle over his back, grabbed the .410, and moved as stealthily as his old legs would allow across the back yard. He paused by the back door, just long enough to send Riley one word: *Upstairs.*

As it should be, the back door was locked, but Katelyn had given them both a copy of the key. Robert unlocked the door and stepped inside.

Riley was already at the bottom of the stairs. She nodded at him and began to ascend.

Robert had thought he'd heard voices as he stepped inside, but now there was nothing but ominous silence as Robert caught up to Riley and they ascended together.

The silence was quickly shattered by a scream and *something* that Robert could only describe as a roar.

They both stopped.

A barrage of noises followed the roar—screams, thuds, howls—and a guitar flew through the door and shattered against the wall above them. They paused, then started up the stairs again, tip-toeing amongst pieces of the guitar.

Robert passed Riley and stepped into the doorway first, and he initially wasn't sure what he saw, wasn't sure if it was real, didn't see how it could be....

But then Riley, from beside him, said, "Oh my God," and he knew it was real.

The dismembered woman on the floor was Katelyn. The shotgun was next to her. Broken open— truly broken, and unfired.

Riley knelt next to her.

Gone. Just *gone*.

The octagon window at the end of the room was broken open. Pieces of its trim were on the floor below it.

Robert went to the window.

For now, it framed the rising moon perfectly.

42

I'LL BE FINE. KEEP YOUR silver bullet.

He'd tried. Really. But, standing there on that god-forsaken "road" in the middle of nowhere, she'd insisted: *There are two. Take one.*

So, Palmer had a silver bullet. It was currently in his shirt pocket. And all day, he'd never once considered actually loading the thing into his gun's magazine. He'd feel like a fool! Even considering everything he'd seen… even considering all that, no. He couldn't do it.

So he'd thought.

But now… Now, he was standing beneath a burnt out lamp just two houses up the street from Katelyn's, watching the full moon creep higher and higher. Now, he had to admit, he was thinking about it. Would it hurt anything?

Yeah, you fool. It could jam your damned gun.

His phone rang. It was Riley.

He listened to her and felt one hell of a lump form in his throat, and he put the phone back in his pocket.

Move, damn it.

It was difficult to find the ability to move, but after the first step was behind him, he quickly broke into a steady jog that took him all the way up Katelyn's yard, where he found Riley and Robert at the east end of the house. Riley was shining a flashlight up at a broken octagon window that hung by one of its two hinges. There were marks—scratches—down the side of the house, too, he noted, visible only in the siding above the bricks.

"Faint prints in the yard," Robert said. "You can tell he went that way." The old man pointed toward the neighbor's back yard. "Everybody in town is in danger."

"Then start telling them," Palmer said.

He was weak. He had to see her. For now, that's all he knew.

He went inside and ascended the stairs. As he went, he called the department and told them to send out an alert that Dean Mitchell had killed his wife and was still out there and should be considered extremely dangerous—television, radio, social media, all of it. He left out the *monster* part.

He sighed and shook his head when he found Katelyn's body. Her face was unrecognizable. Her abdomen was a bleeding crater. Her left arm had been torn from her body and tossed aside.

Palmer went downstairs to call the coroner.

He was sick and fucking tired of calling the coroner.

Robert set off to knock on doors and warn everybody he could find.

Riley attempted to follow Dean Mitchell's (very faint) path, but this proved to be impossible: he hadn't really *left* a path, just a few areas of beaten down grass on the east side of the lawn. Robert had been correct when he said the tracks went generally east…. They just didn't go very far. And there was not a chance in hell of finding any tracks on the other side of the chain-link fence between the lawns.

The neighbor's back yard was mostly dirt, thanks to the seventy-pound husky named Doris that held sway over it.

Doris, Riley noted, was doing fine. The beautiful white and gray dog sat proudly at the base of the back steps, practically glowing in the moonlight.

Riley had her elbows on top of the fence and was staring off into absolutely nothing when Palmer stepped up beside her.

"We're looking," he said. "God almighty damn."

"I hate it."

"Hate isn't enough. That's the worst yet."

"And I'm just standing here."

Two marked cruisers pulled up in front of the house; they were followed by the coroner a moment later.

Palmer went back inside, and Riley walked along the fence.

Doris, she noticed, did not seem to care about her existence at all.

Am I really here? Or did I die in there? Is any of this real?

She went back inside to help Palmer survey the madness.

ROBERT HAD BEEN GONE OVER an hour when he returned to the Mitchells' house at ten till ten. By this time, the house was crawling with law enforcement and medical personnel. Neighbors were on their porches. The full moon hovered above the trees. Too bright. Too close. Forget the haunting, pulsing, swirling reds and blues from the emergency vehicles; forget that every light in the doomed couple's house was on. The moon. That was all.

Riley had stepped out onto the porch with Robert because, yet again, she'd decided she could not stand the suffocating atmosphere within.

"I've been all over Ellingwood, and out of it," Robert said. "I'm now the crazy old guy."

He'd left the deer rifle in his Ranger and was leaning on the .410 like a cane.

Riley descended the front steps and went to the fence. Robert followed.

"If he's out there," Riley said, "somebody will find him. But I don't think he is."

"Why?"

"We're next. Her friends. We know about him." She kept her eyes on Doris. "He knows we're trying to kill him. I think…" What did she think? "He'll try to kill us. He's got a plan."

Doris was still sitting tall in front of the back steps, staring straight ahead at God knows what. Something, Riley assumed, in the trees at the back of the yard.

247

Robert leaned into the fence. "The dog sees something, you think?"

He was answered by an apocalyptic roar and a flash of molten orange, which was followed immediately by a rain of debris.

Riley did not realize she'd hit the ground until Robert was helping her up.

Above them, flames licked at the remains of the blasted wall that had once contained the octagon window.

"Palmer," Robert said. "They were all up there."

The sheriff emerged onto the porch as they rounded the corner of the house. Behind him, the house's interior was blood and screams and fire. The bottom had fallen out, and that's what was left: Blood and screams and fire. Palmer was holding his left leg. His face was a mask of black and red.

He let himself collapse on the front steps. "Amplifier. Remember the shit we found?" He coughed and brought a fist down. "God *damn*!"

Riley stood over him, frantic yet incapable of movement, trying to understand.

Somehow, the world was silent and moving slowly. Nothing, she thought, was real—except it obviously *was*.

A siren emerged from the not-so-distant reaches of the night, then another.

When she found the ability to move again, she stepped out into the yard and called 911 and warned them that it was a bomb, then messaged two members of the volunteer fire department and called the police and fire departments in Harrison.

But none of the machinery had a clue.

She tucked her phone away.

Turning back to the porch, she saw that Palmer was in considerable pain. It was the wound in his leg. He was gritting his teeth as he clutched it; blood oozed between his fingers.

Robert was next to him, using a pocketknife to cut away the bottom two thirds of the sheriff's left pants leg.

A dumbstruck deputy knelt at the end of the porch and attempted to throw up.

"I'm fine," Palmer said. "I'm okay."

He'd been impaled just above the knee by a wedge of thick black plastic as big as a steak knife. The sheriff gritted his teeth and clinched the plastic shard in both hands and closed his eyes as he pulled it from the wound. It resisted with an audible *slurp*.

Riley went inside for towels and peroxide. As she helped Robert with the wound, a dim light came on in the house next door.

Riley handed the towel to Robert and stepped back out into the yard.

Up and down the street, people were on their porches and in their yards. Indeed, after the blast, *everybody* was. Except the neighbor, Doris's owner. Sure, he was an older guy, a loner who lived (as Riley had heard) only for his dog.

Still, he'd surely heard the blast.

"Robert," Riley said.

He looked up, and—

The howl from the neighbor's house strove for the moon.

Robert gave the sheriff a pat on the shoulder and used the shotgun to lift himself up. He hobbled toward Riley on two stiff legs.

From beyond the chain-link fence, Doris dove into a barrage of barks and yelps.

"I'm going over there," Riley said. "Stay with Palmer, he's—"

"He'll live, and deputy boy will take care of him till more help comes. He's got more room for error than we do."

She *could* argue with him, but she didn't. He was right.

Robert collected the backup rifle from his truck, and they crossed to the neighbor's front lawn. Robert followed her past the front walk and the opposite end of the house.

It was remarkably quiet over here, an entirely different world from the inferno just a few hundred feet behind them.

Riley led him through a gate in the fence. Doris's barks and howls had faded to occasional whimpers. And when the dog came into view in the moonlight, they saw that she was still sitting near the steps, staring toward the back of the yard.

Because she's leashed to a concrete block. This was not normal. Riley didn't know the homeowner all that well, but from what she'd seen, Doris always had the run of the yard.

Riley told the dog she'd be okay, and they started toward the back of the yard.

The moon was now so high and bright they didn't need their flashlights, and the homeowner's corpse, dangling Christ-like from the fence by his outstretched arms, was visible long before they reached it.

They stopped ten or so feet from the nightmare.

Robert turned away immediately.

Riley put a hand on his back and looked back at the house.

She recalled the light coming on just moments ago.

Somebody's in there.

And it obviously wasn't the man who was *supposed* to be in there.

"This can't even be *real*," Robert whispered through a throat full of gravel.

Riley squeezed his shoulder, and they proceeded back up the yard. The back door was locked, so they circled around to check the front.

The front door was, strangely, unlocked: the latch moved easily beneath Riley's thumb, and she pushed the door inward slowly, half an inch at a time.

She wasn't foolish. And, because of the bomb, she was probably hypersensitive.

Whatever the reason, she knew something was wrong, even as she opened the door.

And she felt it before it happened.

IT WAS THE BOMB ALL over again, except it wasn't.

This explosion was a sharp *clap* that was over as soon as it was there.

A rifle blast, Robert thought, and it sent Riley flying backwards off the stoop.

He heard himself say her name, and she was sitting up, thank God, before he could so much as step down to her.

She was down in the yard, propped up on one elbow, examining the opposite shoulder.

"Is anybody in there?" she said.

The door was standing a foot open, and from where they were positioned, Robert could squint and just make out the gun on the other side of the room; the crouched, waitingki beast was perched atop the TV cabinet beneath a wall-mounted flat screen.

"Spring gun," he said. "I don't see anybody. Yet."

"What about my shoulder?"

He pulled back the neck of her sweatshirt, revealing a deep gash to the right of her bra strap.

"You felt the wind of that one," he said. "It's gonna sting."

He helped her stand and made sure she was okay— she insisted she was—and took the lead, removing his pocketknife as he knelt down in front of the door. He motioned for Riley to stay back, reached in, and, just to be safe, cut the string attached to the rifle that had nearly blown away a sizable piece of Riley's left shoulder.

Then, with his left foot, Robert nudged the door open, revealing the entirety of the living room. Two lamps were on. The television was off. A bolt-action Winchester was bracketed to the TV cabinet, string tied to the trigger and strung across the floor along a network of protruding screws.

"God knows what else there is," Robert said, admiring the gun.

Riley, left shoulder sagging just a bit, Glock in her left hand, said: "Do you smell that?"

There *was* something oppressive in the air, and it was more than a foul stench.

They moved through the kitchen and dining room. Both were dark and still.

But a door was standing ajar at the other end of the house, at the end of a corridor that branched off the living room. Dim yellow light seeped out of the crack and onto the carpet and walls.

Robert led the way toward the light. He could see it again, the thing coming at him, and he caught its face with the .30-06, but *it hadn't been enough*. Tonight would be enough.

Brave, he thought, *real brave*.

Mere feet from the light, his bravery faded.

He turned.

Riley was behind him. Much of her color had faded, and her sweatshirt's left shoulder was matted with blood.

"I'm okay," she said.

SHE SUPPOSED IT WAS TRUE. She was *fine* in the sense that she was (probably) not going to die from this wound. The bullet had caught the top of her shoulder, not blown through any organs or bone. But it was bleeding insanely, and her shoulder and the side of her neck were going numb. Her head was foggy, too, like she'd been drinking. Adrenaline. A profusely bleeding wound. It was to be expected.

I'm alive. But what's to be done?

253

Robert stepped into the doorway.

My vision's blurry, she thought.

When she blinked, things cleared. At least a little.

She clenched the Glock's grip and wondered if she was capable of firing it. Life wasn't an action movie, and she was no hero. On a good day, she was *maybe* above average with a gun. And this wasn't a *good day.*

Robert entered the room.

Riley followed and moved in front of him.

The light was coming from a tall floor lamp in the corner. Its old-fashioned yellow shade and low wattage bulb cast the room in a dingy, putrid glow. The lamp's pull chain swayed slowly to-and-fro.

The room was bare, containing only a corner desk and a printer on a rolling cart.

"Nothing," Robert said.

It came from the darkness across the hall, and Riley would later blame herself and only herself for what happened to her friend. Even in her foggy state, she should've never let them *both* turn their backs on the opposite bedroom.

The thing grabbed Robert, tore at his neck, and flung him backward. The old man hit the wall next to the door and crumpled to the floor.

Riley rushed toward the lamp, as far away from the thing as she could get. The window was her only escape hatch. But she'd need to raise it and knock out the screen. Too much time. Her chances of putting silver in the thing's face were greater than making it out into the lawn.

She spun around and for the first time saw the monster in all its glory.

It was tall and seemingly frail, though it was anything *but* that. Frayed remnants of a shirt hung from its arms. Its head was canine, its snout perpetually snarling. The fur, which covered it head to toe, was a blend of gray and brown and was matted with God knows what. There was nothing of Dean Mitchell left except—and she wasn't *sure* about this—a faint glimmer of humanity in its eyes.

Perhaps the monster was still processing the fact that neither of its adversaries had been eliminated by the spring gun. Or maybe there was something about her the creature found interesting. Whatever the case, it simply stood there for a long while, looking at her.

Does it want to tell me something?

No.

It covered the distance between them before she could finish raising her gun, and the Glock was flying and the monster was on her. It would have torn out her throat and finished her immediately had she not raised a hand into its face and buried a fingernail in one of its eyes. The resulting howl was humid and smelled like bile. She pressed deeper.

It rose, surely less than an inch, but enough for her to reach out and grab the Glock. She brought the gun in and pressed the end of the barrel into the center of its chest, right below the neck.

It knew immediately what was happening and brought a claw around.

Riley was set to take the blow. Fuck it, it was worth it, because she was about to kill it. She squeezed the trigger—but the bullet did not fire. The round caught between the magazine and the chamber.

The blow struck a split second later. She'd lowered her head and turned it as much as possible before it landed; thus, she caught the thing's knuckles in the side of her face instead of its nails across her throat.

She then adjusted her grip on the gun and brought its butt end up and around, delivering a solid hit to the monster's head. It rose again, Riley attempted to pull away, but it drove her back into the floor with a fist to her ribs.

A fireball exploded below her right breast. Her breath left her, and the room, already foggy, went gray, almost black.

If it would just *get off of her*, she could still chamber the round. She could kill it; even wounded and half out of her mind, she knew she could.

A wave of that humid and reeking breath again washed over her face, and she saw its teeth, just its teeth and the void behind them, and she knew what was coming.

The thunderclap of a rifle vibrated everything around her, and it was gone.

It hit the floor next to her with a weak noise that she couldn't quite call a whimper.

Riley nearly choked on the air that rushed into her lungs. She rose and blinked rapidly to clear her vision and saw Palmer standing back near the doorway.

He was wielding what she thought was Robert's rifle, which was fine for getting the thing off of her, but...

She lumbered out of its reach just as it was rising and reaching for her.

Palmer fired again.

The *boom* nearly brought the room down.

The lamp wavered and the shadows danced in the dingy light.

The wolf was blown backward into the printer cart, and both the monster and the machine hit the floor.

Good. But not enough.

A deputy appeared in the doorway; he went wide-eyed and fell into the frame.

The creature hurled the printer at Palmer. The sheriff sidestepped and ducked and obviously had no idea what his next move should be. He'd hit the thing twice at close range with a rifle that could easily drop an elk or a bear.

And the inhuman bastard was getting up again.

Riley positioned herself beside him and thought about going for the .410, but they were so close to the creature that any move could be lethal, especially one that involved crossing nearly the entire floor.

"The silver bullet," Riley said.

"Jammed. Grabbed this off of Robert. Didn't want to hit you with the scatter gun."

The wolf locked eyes with Palmer, then turned and knocked most of the bedroom window out with a single swing of its right arm. It was pushing itself through the window's wreckage when Palmer fired again. But he was visibly shaking, and the shot went wide to the right as the beast fled into the night.

Riley pushed past Palmer and the deputy, scooping Robert's shotgun off the floor as she did so.

There were several dumbstruck people standing along the edge of the yard—out of the way, thank God.

257

Riley pushed on, out of the house, out into the street, wincing with every step, wondering how she was going to catch the thing, stop, aim the shotgun…

None of it mattered.

She stopped less than fifty yards from the house and let the gun fall to her side.

The monster, once again, was gone.

43

A KNOCK ON HER DOOR.

Riley's winced as she rose from the dining table. She was better. That was undeniable. But *better* didn't mean a whole lot.

She found Palmer on her front porch and managed a slight smile.

"You're alive," he said. "Glad to see you."

She stepped aside and let him enter.

He removed his hat and followed her into the dining room.

She offered him a drink as she poured herself an iced tea.

He declined and sat across from her and watched her drink hers.

"Four days," Palmer said when she finally made eye contact. "Still nothing."

"I know."

"You're not out searching today."

"I'm trying a different tactic."

She did not add that this new tactic was closely related to exhaustion, pain, and wine.

"You've got every right to take some time," he said. "It's chaos out there. Talked to a guy this morning from CNN. No kidding. This thing's catching on. Take a break from it, just don't kick yourself. I've seen how you've been the last two days."

"I didn't protect either of the people I meant to protect."

"Katelyn was doomed and Robert chose to go with you."

"I should've *never* left Katelyn that day. He'd obviously killed in broad daylight, but I got caught up in the moon business and thought I had a *minute*. I should have never let Robert go in. I should've known to check the other bedroom."

"It's an unbelievable mess. A Navy Seal wouldn't have handled it any better or done more."

"I'm fine, just thinking. Driving around and wandering all day isn't working."

Palmer drummed his fingers on the table. "Please be okay, Riley." He reached across the table and took her hand. "Sorry I doubted you."

SHE'D BEEN READING. THE ADRENALINE rush of the last full moon had faded. The proverbial battle had been lost, but it was time to return to the books and win the war. She wasn't sure Palmer would agree with her studious approach. The machinery was too stuck in its ways. For them, despite everything Palmer had seen, this was still a *manhunt*. But Dean Mitchell was no human.

So, last night, amidst a wine-induced fog, she'd dipped back into *Folklore of the Full Moon*, reread all those pages about Idalia and lycanthropy, and something—if she could remember her own (blurry) thoughts—had come to her during her second time through the text.

She shut the door behind Palmer and locked it and returned to the dining room with her laptop. She poured another glass of tea and sat down in front of the computer and read it all again.

Was there hope?

Was *she* okay?

She went to the bathroom and faced the mirror.

The bastard had only delivered two solid hits. One to the side of her face, the other to her chest.

Her face was already much improved. There was a row of tender markings along her right jaw, but the swelling had gone down and the colors were fading.

She pulled off her sweatshirt, knowing what she was going to see but needing to check again, anyway.

The gash on her shoulder still burned, but it was healing. It was the explosion of swollen color on the right side of her body that was truly crippling. It still hurt to breathe deeply. She could only sleep on her back. Forget coughing. Forget laughing. Forget putting any pressure on any part of her stomach, ribcage, or right boob. Bras? No. Only this worn-out Walmart sports bra was remotely tolerable.

Still, she was lucky. The thing had been on top of her. And she was alive. Beaten. Sore. *But not scratched.*

261

She put her sweatshirt back on.

The book had described an alleged "personal account" of a man who'd survived a werewolf attack. He'd taken only a cut to the face before escaping the beast by diving into a lake. After this, he'd claimed the monster had a mental hold on him. The man committed suicide less than a month after the attack. *The result of a cut or scratch from a werewolf is linked to its severity*, the author had claimed. *Concerning wounds that do not result in a total infection of lycanthropy, it seems possible that psychic connections exist between the creatures and their victims.*

Why did this matter? Certainly, Riley wasn't worried about *herself*. She'd just confirmed (for at least the third time) that the thing had not drawn blood from her. She was battered and bruised and *shot*, and she wouldn't be totally normal again for weeks or months (if ever), but (assuming this old book was correct) she was not in danger of having her mind controlled by the monster that was Dean Mitchell.

She left the bathroom and returned to her computer.

SHE STEPPED OUT OF HER house for the first time that day at two 'o clock in the afternoon. She was dressed casually in jeans and a long-sleeve tee shirt and had pulled a ponytail through the back of a baseball cap. She wasn't going anywhere as a constable. Not today.

A young man in khaki pants and a tucked in collared shirt stood near her Jeep.

Thank God her shotgun was already in the back seat and not in her hands. She certainly wasn't in the mood to deal with *that*.

"I'm with the Southeastern *Telegram*," the young man said. "My paper is out of El Dorado. I've come a long way. Are you Constable Riley Saunders?"

"I am." She circled around to the driver's door. "I'm not talking, I'm sorry."

"But you were there. Is it true Mr. Mitchell is some sort of monster? Surely you understand that—"

She got in her Jeep, shut the door, and started the engine.

SHE PASSED TWO MARKED CHARGERS on her way out of town. They were pulled over on the side of the highway, their drivers no doubt out in the weeds somewhere, probably finding nothing. And so what if they did find him? What did they think they were going to do?

Three miles north of the Ellingwood line, Riley slowed from fifty-five to less than thirty miles an hour. She had no idea how well Deer Creek Road was marked. Finding Doctor Amanda Smelter's address had been as simple as a Google search, but applying the contents of the Internet to reality wasn't always straightforward.

Thankfully, Deer Creek Road, a decent but narrow stretch of packed gravel, was marked with an upright, traditional county road sign. Riley made the left and quickly covered the four miles to the quaint little "community" of Deer Creek—a spread-out cluster of upscale homes on the banks of the namesake creek.

Smelter's house was a two-story cabin in the center of several mowed and perfectly landscaped acres.

Riley parked behind the silver Audi, closed her eyes, and took a deep breath.

She'd taken three Advil before leaving the house, but it still hurt to climb out of the Jeep. Even the modest efforts required to grab the shotgun from the backseat and her lock pick set from the compartment beneath the driver's seat sent tiny threads of pain through her back and stomach.

Focus.

But it was hard to focus, because she still felt just a little bit crazy.

She probably always would.

She knocked on the front door and rang the bell. Nobody answered. Palmer had talked to Smelter twice since the full moon. Riley had talked to her once. The doctor had looked and sounded sick.

There were a million different reasons why she wouldn't answer the door.

Riley trusted none of them.

She tried the doorbell one more time. Nothing.

The door was locked, but she had it unlocked in less than two minutes.

She tucked the lock pick set into her back pocket, entered Smelter's home with both hands on the shotgun, and nudged the door shut with one foot.

She found herself totally immersed in staples of the American middle class: Tile entryway. Hardwood floors. High ceilings. Leather furniture. Granite countertops.

But Riley didn't give a damn about home decor.

She did not call out to Smelter. She was done with announcing her presence, and the feeling that she was right and something was *wrong* was practically tangible.

She cocked the silver-loaded .410 and set out into the first floor. *Surely* the shotgun shell would not fail. But if it did, her Glock was tucked away securely under the band of her tee shirt.

In reality, there wasn't a damn thing to shoot, not on the first floor, anyway. Kitchen, dining room, living room, master bedroom, bathrooms… All empty, all quiet. Televisions off. Laptop closed on the coffee table. No sign of life at all.

So she proceeded to the stairs and stood at the bottom, gazing up into the quiet gray.

Chances are, she thought, *there is nobody here. Yes, her car is outside, but so what? She could be out with a friend.*

Or dead.

Riley ascended as softly as possible, taking the treads two at a time.

Close to the top, a foul odor brushed her nose. And on the landing, she knew it: he was here.

It made sense, didn't it? The *Folklore* book had triggered the idea that he'd somehow established a connection with Smelter, hence her showing up the night before the full moon. And if he'd used her to get out, why wouldn't he use her for refuge?

Riley hadn't been sure, until now.

Now, she'd either do what needed to be done, or she would join the friends she'd failed.

From the landing, there was only one way to go. Right.

Three doors opened off of this corridor, and she found what she was looking for behind the first one.

Dean Mitchell and Amanda Smelter were lying in bed, the covers and comforter pulled up to their chins. Neither appeared healthy. Both were ghostly gray. If not for the slight rise and fall of the sheets, Riley would think them dead.

She quietly crossed the floor to the doctor's side of the bed. She kept one hand on the shotgun and used the other to pull the covers back from Smelter's body. Riley doubted she could get Amanda out of the bed without waking Mitchell. But she had to come as close to that as possible.

She'd exposed Smelter down to her waist when the doctor's eyes blinked a few times, then went wide. She didn't scream, thank goodness—maybe she *couldn't*.

Riley put a finger to her lips and motioned for Smelter to get off the bed.

The doctor barely knew who or where she was, but she threw her legs over the side. And Riley couldn't believe the sight of her. How long had it been since Smelter had been up and around? They'd talked to her three days ago; she'd met them at the sheriff's office. So it couldn't have been *that* long. But the shape of her was embossed in the mattress. The white tee shirt she wore was transparent with sweat, and both the smell of the room and the appearance of her panties and the sheets indicated this successful, highly intelligent woman had somehow lost the drive—or ability—to go to the bathroom.

Her right hand was swollen with infection.

Before Riley could help her stand, Dean Mitchell's good eye fluttered and opened and rolled in her direction. She had no idea if he saw her, though. The eye was blank.

Riley remained calm. She put a hand on Smelter's back and urged her out of the bed. But damnation! The woman was oblivious and would not take the hint.

Mitchell started to rise.

Riley gave Smelter a hard shove, and the doctor half rose and half stumbled into the floor.

Riley retreated to the foot of the bed and, with painful effort, raised the shotgun.

Mitchell, like Smelter, seemed to be unaware of his situation, at least for a few seconds. He searched for reason, one eye rolling madly, the other a glossy bulb of swollen flesh, as he sat up and the sheets and comforter fell away.

Then that mad eye found her, and all confusion vacated his face.

God help her, he grinned.

And reached beneath his pillow.

"You fucking bitch," he said.

Riley saw the gun and did not give him a chance to aim. She pulled the trigger.

At such close range, Dean Mitchell did not stand a chance. His head absorbed, and was effectively obliterated by, the force of the .410 blast and the silver pellets contained within it.

The pistol fell from his hand.

The contents of his head splattered the wall and bed.

His upper torso slumped back against the headboard and was still.

Riley lowered the shotgun and leaned back against the wall. The entire right side of her body throbbed. She was shaking.

She slid down to the floor and told herself not to lose it. Amanda Smelter was slumped gainst the closet door, dirty, oblivious, and splattered with Dean Mitchell's gore.

God knows what the poor woman had been through these last two or three days.

Hopefully she'd remember none of it.

He's dead.

For now, that's what mattered. For Katelyn and for Robert. For everybody else, too.

Riley crawled across the floor to Amanda Smelter and told her she'd be okay.

Then she found the strength to stand and step out into the hallway.

It was time to call Palmer and tell him it was, hopefully, over.

August 1, 2017

Author's Note

Thanks so much for reading *Folklore*. The werewolf tale is nearly as old as fiction itself, but it was fun throwing my own entry into the lycanthropy canon.

Honest reviews mean the world to me. If you get a chance, please consider posting your thoughts about the book on Amazon or Goodreads.

Most importantly, again: thanks for reading.

Mitch Sebourn

Twitter: @mnsebourn
www.mitchsebourn.com

Made in the USA
Monee, IL
21 January 2023

25867775R00163